William Dutton Burrard

A great platonic friendship

Vol. I

William Dutton Burrard

A great platonic friendship
Vol. I

ISBN/EAN: 9783743373815

Manufactured in Europe, USA, Canada, Australia, Japa

Cover: Foto ©Andreas Hilbeck / pixelio.de

Manufactured and distributed by brebook publishing software (www.brebook.com)

William Dutton Burrard

A great platonic friendship

A GREAT PLATONIC FRIENDSHIP.

VOL. I.

NEW AND POPULAR NOVELS

A GREAT

PLATONIC FRIENDSHIP

BY

W. DUTTON BURRARD

IN THREE VOLUMES.

VOL. I.

LONDON:

HURST AND BLACKETT, LIMITED,

13, GREAT MARLBOROUGH STREET.

1887.

DEDICATED

TO

MY FRIEND AND COMRADE,

ARTHUR DAVIDSON YOUNG,

WHO,

DURING MY SOJOURN UNDER HIS KINDLY ROOF,

IN A FAR-OFF HYMALAYAN HUT,

UNCONSCIOUSLY, BY HIS OWN ACTION, GENERATED IN ME

THE FIRST GERMS OF THE

GREAT PLATONIC FRIENDSHIP.'

CONTENTS

OF

THE FIRST VOLUME.

———

A GREAT PLATONIC FRIENDSHIP.

CHAPTER I.

AT THE CLUB.

IT is August, and the sun is shining brightly down upon the Doonga Hill. For several days the station has been wrapped in a robe of impenetrable mist, which has caused much discontent amongst the inhabitants, who, after months spent in the broiling heat of the plains, have come up to the Himalayas to recoup their health with reinvigorating draughts of pure mountain air.

The constant fog, which has penetrated to every corner in every house, has had a most depressing effect on the inmates of fair Doonga, and all talk of coming gaieties and social excitements has latterly ceased, and has given way to lugubrious platitudes regarding the state of the weather. But in the Doonga Club the effect has been even more disastrous, for the gay young bachelors temporarily inhabiting its virtuous precincts have day and night drowned dull care in foaming bumpers of champagne, resulting in the very hardest hands confessing to feeling a trifle shaky.

But now at last the sun has burst through the mass of cloud, and has dispersed it to the winds, and the peaks of the neighbouring hills appear again on all sides, looking very charming in the soft morning light.

Several young men, dressed for the most part in flannel *déshabille*, are lounging about the verandah of the club, wearing on their pallid faces a look of intense *ennui*, which all the brilliant panorama stretched before their eyes has no power to disperse, for they feel that shattered nerves, such as theirs are on this particular morning, require, to regain their normal vigour of action, a more stimulating pick-me-up than the sight of a glorious stretch of mountain scenery.

There has been a very big drink the night before, and the card-room has been in request till very late in the morning,

and the effect of their past conviviality is
now plainly imprinted on their despairing
faces. To them now life is unutterably
hollow, and they move about the verandah
with a listless sense of apathy, uttering at
times monosyllabic ejaculations of more
force than polish, as though to walk and
talk were positive exertions.

With supreme indifference they cast
their eyes down far beneath them to the
mountain stream which looks to them, by
reason of its distance, merely a thin streak
of bright light, but which is in reality,
from the effects of the recent rains, a swollen torrent, lashing itself furiously along
its rugged bed. Then, with an expression
of intense weariness, they lift their heads,
and gaze upwards at the sky, and sigh
sadly, as the warm rays play upon their
faces. They are glad, in a listless kind of
way, that the weather has changed at last,
but at present they are hardly in a fit state
to truly appreciate the charms of warmth
and sunshine. In fact, many of them experience a feeling of positive injury towards
the fiery Phœbus in not having intimated
to them the day before his intention of appearing again so soon, so as to have given

them twenty-four hours' grace to pull themselves together in order to be able to enjoy
his gladdening presence.

'Just the sort of shabby trick it *would*
play, you know!' murmurs somebody, in a
surly tone of voice, throwing himself down
disconsolately into a low arm-chair. 'What
have we done to deserve such a cursed fate
as this? With a sick headache and a
clammy tongue, life is certainly *not* worth
living.'

No one attempts to answer him, the
company assembled deeming it advisable,
considering the circumstances, to accept
without challenge his dogmatic utterance.

Conversation rises and falls in fits and
starts, and it is not of an edifying character.
The revelry of the night before is the chief
topic which occupies their minds, and each
member severally recalls, in a diffident
manner, some speech or incident of remarkable wit and humour, in which he has
played the primary part.

Then follows a long silence, during
which the members of this little circle of
used-up individuals gaze dismally into each
other's faces, perfectly incapable of framing
one single thought coherently.

There is something comical in the sorrowful aspect which they present, lying loosely about the place, in various attitudes suggestive of despair. And so it strikes young Loftus of the Light Dragoons, who, in direct contrast to those surrounding him, is sitting, fresh and bright, on the seat in the verandah, facing his disconsolate companions.

'What devils we are!' he murmurs, abstractedly, pensively stroking his moustache, concealing by the action a faint flicker of a smile.

'Yes, I think we can raise hell, if we have a mind to,' says Bramley, the orator, with immense self-complacency.

There is a murmur of acquiescence from those around him, and then another silence, depressing in intensity, falls upon the company.

Presently Loftus remarks that, curiously enough, he is feeling rather dry, so he proceeds to call for a whisky-peg, at which several others follow suit, resolving rather to die than to show to their more hardened companion that they are feeling the effects of the night before. Oh! what a noble ambition! To thirst for notoriety as a hard-

liver and drinker! How can one say that
the spirit of manliness is extinct in the
human race?

They drink their pegs in solemn silence,
Loftus marking with inward amusement
the vain attempts of many to appear to
enjoy them. A diversion presently arises.
The noise of coolies, passing beneath them,
strikes upon their ears, and, from their slip-
shod method of progression, they know that
some one is being carried up the hill in a
dandy—a species of canoe, supported on
long bamboos, which serves in the place of
a carriage in this part of the Himalayas.

'I wonder who it is?' says the orator,
apathetically, without making an effort to
discover.

Loftus turns round, and leans over the
balcony, and gazes at the approaching
dandy. It contains a lady of slender figure,
whose face, however, he is unable to see on
account of her open parasol. But Loftus is
not a man to be deterred by trifles. He
gives vent to a little cough to attract the
lady's attention, and his ruse succeeds, for
the parasol is lowered, but only for an
instant. In another moment it is raised
again with a sudden jerk, but not before

Loftus has had time to scan a face of almost perfect loveliness. With a blank expression he stares after the retreating dandy, and then a low whistle of astonishment issues from his lips.

'Diana Forsdyke, by all that's holy !' he exclaims, slowly. 'What in the name of wonder has brought her again to Doonga?'

'What ! Do you know the nymph?' says Bramley.

'Know her !' he answers, sharply, 'who does not know Diana Forsdyke? By gad ! she is a deep one, if you like ! Now, I wonder what that volatile young woman's game is just at present?'

A look of interest settles on many of the pallid faces, and there is a general murmur of inquiry for further particulars. But Loftus suddenly retires within his shell, and makes a most ungracious reply.

'Curse it !' he says. 'If you chaps want to know, go and ask her yourselves. It is not *my* business to enlighten you as to her private affairs.'

The atmosphere of gloom returns. No one attempts to question Loftus further, for they one and all, in their inmost hearts, acknowledge him as a superior being in that he is capable of drinking the best of them under the table without turning a hair. So they relapse once more into silent melancholy, and inwardly curse their fate in having been born into such a truly second-rate sort of world.

The sound of a bugle suddenly re-echoes through the hills, and every man in the verandah jumps to his feet, and peers anxiously down the road. To these *blasés*, wearied spirits, accustomed as they were to begin the day by wishing it were over, the prospect of a new arrival from the plains is sufficient to rouse them for the moment from their usual despondent state. It is a real excitement, for, though there be nothing peculiarly stimulating in the sight of a new face, still it *is* new, and that is the main point, for they craved for novelty day and night.

Every face is turned in eager expectation towards the cart-road leading down to Pindi, but nothing comes in sight. Groups of coolies are hustling together at the tonga-terminus. They too have heard the sound, and the prospect of obtaining a few *pice* has roused them from the solemn discussion which they have been holding round a mud-

begrimed hubble-bubble. They have dropped the bond of fraternity, and are now
standing in bitter enmity towards each
other, waiting eagerly for the coming
prey.

Again the broken bugle sounds, now
harsh and painful by reason of its close
proximity, and presently the tonga appears
at full gallop, drawn by a pair of country-
breds of the usual doubtful condition. The
driver cracks his whip across their bony
backs, and the little vehicle dashes up the
hill, coming to a sudden halt before the
tonga-office. The ponies stand with heaving flanks in a bath of steam, the driver
dismounts, the coolies push and clamour
round the cart, all jabbering loudly in their
outlandish tongue, and confusion reigns
supreme.

From above, these proceedings have
been observed with the greatest interest,
and now every eye is gazing expectantly
for the coming man. At last he alights—
a tall, slim figure, wrapped closely up in
a thick ulster, with a well-set head surmounted by a shooting-cap. Surmises as
to whom and what he is, and criticisms on
his general appearance, fall thick and fast,

and for a moment the dull apathy of the verandah has entirely disappeared.

'By Jove! this *is* a pleasant surprise!' exclaims Loftus, suddenly. 'If it isn't Grandby, of all people in the world!'

'Who the devil's Grandby?' growls the orator, in a surly tone, feeling keenly at a disadvantage, and determined consequently not to display too much interest in the subject.

'Why—Grandby of the Gunners—I knew him well at home. He is only a young chap, but he used to be an awfully good sort—up to any lark.'

'Then bring him up here, for heaven's sake, and let him try to put a little life in us,' is the irritable rejoinder. 'Though, for the matter of that, he does not seem to possess too much of that commodity himself.'

'No, by gad, more he does, poor chap! Well, I will just trot down and have a look at him.'

Loftus quickly leaves the verandah, and the rest of the company begin to discuss the likelihood of Grandby being a match for Loftus in the art of drinking to excess without suffering from the effects

of the carouse. The younger portion are
prepared to receive the new-comer with
open arms; for has not Loftus designated
him 'an awfully good sort,' and are they
not ready to follow Loftus in his every
opinion to the death?

In the meanwhile, Grandby, quite oblivious to the excitement which his arrival
has caused amongst the tortured beings up
above in the club verandah, having dis-
mounted from the tonga, stretches his
stiffened limbs, and then looks around at
the mass of dirty coolies fighting and gesti-
culating on all sides. He makes a sign to
them to remove his travelling-bag from the
cart, and in a moment a dozen naked forms
have pounced upon it like a pack of hungry
wolves. Seeing his personal property in
imminent danger of being torn to shreds,
he forces his way into the ragged crowd,
and takes it in hand and gives it to a small
boy, who has been standing silently on the
outskirts of the struggling mass, thus unconsciously reversing the old adage, 'That
to him that hath shall be given, but to
him that hath not shall be taken away even
that which he hath!'

A loud groan of disappointment follows

on the movement, but, nothing daunted, Grandby, having given instructions concerning his heavy baggage, orders the boy to march.

'Banbury's Hotel,' he says, and, turning round, he finds himself face to face with Loftus, whom he has known more or less intimately in England.

'How are you, Grandby? How are you, old chap? Saw you from the verandah above, and came down in three shakes of a bumble-bee's tail. But, by gad, sir, you are looking devilish seedy. What have you been doing to yourself—you are as white as a sheet!'

'How are you, Loftus?' says Grandby, shaking him by the hand. 'I have had a fearful go of fever down below, so they have had to send me up here on sick-leave. I shall soon pick up, I trust, in this delightful climate.'

'Delightful! do you call it?' says Loftus, with a shudder of disgust. 'You are the first man whom I have heard say that for many a long week. But come on up to the club! We will make you pretty jolly there before long, I bet.'

'No, thanks. I am up here for rest and

quiet, and I know the club by hearsay. It wouldn't suit me, I am afraid.'

'What bosh, my dear sir! If there be a place to pick a poor devil up, it is the club. The wines are really magnificent.'

'I don't doubt it,' returns Grandby, with a short laugh; 'but I have already made my plans. I am going to Banbury's Hotel.'

'Great—heavens!' ejaculates Loftus, with tremendous energy. 'What a truly terrible idea! Why, you will be dead from sheer *ennui* befor dinner-time to-night! Now, look here, really, old chap'—relapsing suddenly into the confidential—' you *must* reconsider your decision. Banbury's is as dull as ditch-water, and twice as un-appetising to a young bachelor of your stamp, while in the club, towards the small hours in the morning, there is really a cer-tain amount of life, at times. Yes—I think we can show you, Grandby, the proper way to live. You remember, when we were to-gether at Canterbury four years ago—you used to come over and see us at the barracks —well, we used to play hell then pretty tidily, I think; but it was nothing to the life we lead here, I can assure you. This licks all record.'

A shade of annoyance crosses the open countenance of Frank Grandby. He has known Loftus but slightly in the days to which he refers. His own home had been four miles from the cavalry depôt, and it was through his sister's marriage with a young brother-officer of Loftus' that he had made the acquaintance of the regiment. He was then only a boy of eighteen, and, though he had become very popular in the mess, he had never conceived any great liking for several of the officers, and Loftus in particular had been distasteful to him. Their dispositions were so totally distinct—his being of a peculiarly reserved nature, whilst Loftus was one of those noisy, effervescing men, incapable of any depth of feeling, but ready to chum at a moment's notice with any chance comer.

To Grandby such a course of proceeding was incomprehensible. When he liked, he liked warmly, and was not ashamed to disclose his liking to the world at large, but his nature was totally incapable of affecting an affectionate manner towards those with whom he possessed nothing in common, and to whom he was, in consequence, perfectly indifferent. His pride, too, was as great as his reserve, and accordingly he resented all undue familiarity from those with whom he had no inclination to be familiar.

And so the 'old chappie' style of address adopted by Loftus somewhat jars against his nerves, and he is unable to repress a slight feeling of annoyance, in spite of his conscience urging him not to be so foolish.

He answers rather coldly to Loftus's outburst.

'I am afraid that I cannot alter my plans, Loftus, even to have the pleasure of seeing you raise the infernal regions,'— this a trifle sarcastically. 'You say that Banbury's is dull, so it will just suit me, as I am at present in want of no excitement. And now I really must be off! I suppose that we shall meet again soon.'

'Well, you *are* a pig-headed sort of chap!' cries Loftus, in disgust. 'However, you must not go without having a peg.'

Again he experiences the momentary jar, and it decides him to refuse the offer, which he otherwise might have accepted. Loftus gazes at him for a moment with a look of the blankest amazement depicted on his face. He can hardly believe that he has heard aright. In his own creed, to refuse a drink is a social crime of the deadliest order !

'What !' he gasps, 'you—refuse ?'

Grandby cannot forbear from laughing at the agitated face presented before him.

'I am really not thirsty,' he remarks, by way of apology.

'Not thirsty !' cries Loftus, excitedly ; 'what the deuce has that to do with it ? *Surely* you don't drink only because you are thirsty ?'

'Yes, I do,' answers Grandby, lightly, a smile of amusement on his face : 'is it really such a very extraordinary proceeding ? And now I am off—so, good-bye till we meet again.'

He turns away, and his tall, slim figure moves slowly up the hill, leaving Loftus standing in the middle of the road, the picture of consternation. Such an idea as Grandby has just propounded, regarding the all-important subject of *drink*, is so totally opposed to his own ideas upon the matter that for the moment he stares blankly before him, incapable of action. Then he shakes his head slowly from side to side, and mutters a sentence which by this time is cut and dried:

'Alas! the army is going to the dogs!'

CHAPTER II.

FRANK GRANDBY.

FRANK GRANDBY, preceded by the little grimy sprite with the gladstone-bag, walks slowly up the hill in the direction of Banbury's Hotel.

His progress is not rapid. So unaccustomed is he to the exertion of climbing that more than once he has to stop and rest, in order to regain his breath. For the last two years he has been in the plains, unable to obtain a day's leave, in consequence of his battery, as is the usual case with the Artillery, not being up to its full strength of officers ; and consequently the highest elevation to which he has mounted, since his arrival in the country, has been the top step in the verandah of the Royal Artillery mess at Dhobipur.

It had been exceptionally hot weather this summer at Dhobipur, and Grandby had found himself, to his great disgust, again the only subaltern in the battery, without a prospect of leave. So pocketing his disappointment, as April arrived without the appearance of the long-looked-for brother-officer, he had made up his mind to make the best of a bad thing, and to accept what was inevitable in as contented a spirit as was possible under the circumstances.

Fortunately, however, towards the middle of July, after having borne the brunt of the summer in good health, he was stricken down with such a severe attack of fever that he was utterly incapacitated for work; and after a short struggle to obtain the mastery over the demon, malaria, he passively succumbed, and retired on the sick-list, where he lay for some weeks at certain intervals in high fever.

The medical officer began to look grave. His knowledge of the science of medicine was not so comprehensive as might have been wished, but, as his books of reference prescribed quinine for malaria fever, he began to dose Grandby with that tonic.

And he continued to do so for several weeks, but without the least effect, which was most embarrassing to the poor army-surgeon, for this defiance on the part of the fever in the face of the very highest authority in his medical world was a contingency not admitted in his book of reference, and he was consequently quite at his wit's end what to do. If, he argued to himself, the malady refused to yield to Surgeon-General Upton's famous prescription, then there could be no doubt that it was a case of a most aggravated and serious character.

And there was another cause, too, apart from the low condition of his patient, which gave him much anxiety, and that was that his store of quinine was fast diminishing, and after the repeated injunctions which he had received from head-quarters as to his being very sparing in the issue of that valuable tonic, on the score of expense, the fact naturally caused him no little perturbation of mind. The possibility of his being officially accused of wilful extravagance rose up before him like some grim spectre, and rapidly assumed such awful proportions that he became intensely unhappy in consequence.

But clearly the time for action of a decided character had arrived, for day by day the quinine was being swallowed in alarming quantities, and without the slightest perceptible result. And then came the most horrible thought of all, that possibly, were there to be an official investigation into the abnormally large issue of quinine for the month, he might be ordered to refund its value. It was more than possible —it was probable, the government having a distinct partiality for curtailing its officers' pay, no matter how trifling the excuse or how untenable the claim, keeping for this very purpose, as it does, a band of officials, delicately designated as Pay*examiners*.

This idea was so very painful to the poor surgeon's mind that he summoned up all his courage, and ventured, *for the first time in his life*, to give a professional opinion, which was to the effect that nothing would cure Grandby of the insidious disease but change of air, and that it was absolutely essential that he should go on sick-leave at once.

There was a good deal of opposition to

the proposal. The brigade-surgeon utterly scouted such a preposterous idea, stating in most vehement language that in his opinion the continuance of the disease was due solely to the inefficiency of the medical officer in attendance, whilst the major in command of Grandby's battery announced that the idea was manifestly impossible, for it would leave him without a junior officer of any description whatever. Then there was a demi-official meeting, at which all three aired their various opinions, each one refusing to yield his ground one atom in deference to the other two.

In the course of the proceedings the brigade-surgeon, who had a habit of concealing his own professional incapacity by the adoption of a blustering flow of words, became unmistakably offensive, and Major Grant, who was a man of slow perception, gradually began to become aware that the exalted position which he held as an officer enjoying a distinct command was being overlooked. Such a state of affairs was not to be countenanced for one moment, so the gallant major swerved suddenly round like a weather-cock in a high wind, and boldly announced that he thoroughly agreed with Surgeon O'Brien, in that his subaltern required change of air, stating that it would make no difference whatever to the working of his battery, as, in his opinion, a subaltern officer would be equally efficient in the Himalayas as lying on his back in his room in the agonies of high fever. On hearing this, Surgeon O'Brien, who had been sitting throughout the interview pale with terror, suddenly plucked up spirit, and even had the courage to adopt an official tone of speech, in which he stated that, the case in question being of too grave a nature to be left in the hands of a medical officer of junior rank, he would request the brigade-surgeon to relieve him of it, and to consider the patient, for the future, under his immediate charge. He concluded his remarks by mentioning that, unless this course were adopted, he would not hold himself responsible for what might follow, and then once more his face assumed a look of haggard misery.

The brigade-surgeon was staggered at such stupendous presumption on the part of his subordinate, and inwardly determined to seize on the first opportunity which oc-

curred with an opening for retaliation. To
tell the truth, he found himself in a most
unpleasant position, for he saw that it was
impossible to ignore the gravity of his
junior's statement with Major Grant sitting
there, smouldering wrathfully, a witness to
the whole affair. So the only two lines
open to him were either to give his consent
to Grandby's sick-leave or to accept the
responsibility of the case.

But to this latter alternative there arose
in his eyes a literally insuperable objection,
which was that he lived at the furthest end
of cantonments, which would consequently
oblige him to drive four miles twice a day
in the burning sun in order to see his
patient. The brigade-surgeon was fat, and
was partial to punkah and pygamas, so this
consideration practically decided the question, and after a great deal of unnecessary
bluster, in which he showed his superiority
over Major Grant by delivering an address
of twenty minutes' duration, couched in the
most technical of phraseology, he yielded.
Shortly afterwards, a board assembled to
report on the state of health of Lieutenant
Grandby, and he was speedily despatched
to Doonga on three months' sick-leave.

Two months later, it may be remarked, Surgeon O'Brien was appointed to do duty with the troop-trains taking drafts backward and forward between Peshawur and Bombay, at which horrible occupation he was kept throughout the greater portion of the cold weather. The mention of this circumstance is quite irrelevant, for one would hardly have the hardihood to accuse a full-blown brigade-surgeon of having been guilty of such reprehensible conduct as that of utilising his official power for the gratification of his personal spite. No, I should think not—*veritas odium parit!*

There were two reasons why Frank Grandby chose Doonga in preference to any other hill-station; firstly, because it was close to Dhobipur, and, secondly, because his dear old school-friend, George Grafton, of the Engineers, had written to him, telling him that it was his intention to proceed there, for a few weeks, later on in the year.

The prospect of meeting Grafton again, with whom, in the old days, he had lived on terms of the closest intimacy, was very pleasing to Grandby's mind, and it was with this idea, rather than on account of the state of his health, that he decided to go to Banbury's Hotel, for it was there that Grafton had notified his intention of stopping. Their friendship for one another had been of a character not often met with now-a-days. There were no flaws in the perfect harmony which existed between them, for their affection for one another was perfectly disinterested, and had arisen quite spontaneously in their hearts, without an effort on their parts to create it.

In the old days, when they were boys together at Clifton College, Grafton, who was three years the senior of the two, had taken young Grandby under his protection, and had moulded him according to his own ideas of excellence; and Grandby had looked up to him as to a superior being, and had obeyed him implicitly in all things, feeling intuitively that whatever Grafton did must of necessity be right. And he was correct in his youthful estimate of his mentor's character; for Grafton was possessed of a nature incapable of deceit or wrong, honest, open-hearted, noble-minded, and in all things thorough to the core. And as the years flew by, changing their relative positions as pupil and teacher, and bringing them gradually to an equality, as far as

years and mental development were concerned, a deep affection towards one another
grew within their breasts, and, on the night
of Grafton's departure from school for ever,
they swore to one another, come what may,
to be friends for life.

This was, of course, during that most delightful period of a man's life when it is
possible for him to live in an atmosphere
of romantic friendship with those of his own
sex, perfectly happy and contented, and
wishing for nothing further in the world;
when the heart is fresh and young, impulsive, warm, impressionable, oblivious to the
bitterness and sordid cares of mundane life,
which together dry up all the tenderness
of human nature, causing the human mind
to view all things with cynicism or indifference.

But their friendship was built on too
firm a foundation to be easily shaken, and
the winds and the storms of the fleeting
years were unable to make the least impression on the feeling which they bore to
one another. On the contrary, as they
grew older, and their minds became more
fully formed, they began to appreciate at
its true worth the perfect beauty of a pure,

disinterested friendship, such as theirs was, and the knot which they had loosely tied as boy and boy was re-tied with a stronger hand as man and man.

On leaving school Grafton had joined the Royal Military Academy, and he had already obtained his commission in the Engineers before Grandby entered that establishment. He was, in fact, on the point of sailing for India when Grandby passed his entrance-examination, and the last words they said to one another were, 'We shall meet soon again in India.'

But Fate had not shown herself kind in this particular. Four years had passed, of which Grandby had spent two in Hindostan, but they had never been able to effect a meeting. They had written regularly long letters, detailing all the *minutiæ* of their respective lives; for they were fully alive to the fact that no friendship, however strong, can survive a long separation, unless the parties concerned use every means in their power to keep their memories fresh in each other's mind; but they had never been able to look into each other's face, or to clasp each other's hand. So it may be easily understood what a glad

day it was for Grandby when he found
himself on the way to Doonga, with the
immediate prospect of meeting his old
friend again.

Frank Grandby was possessed of a beautiful face. This epithet is one not generally adopted in the description of a man's
personal appearance, but it is the only one
that will adequately express the charm of
his open countenance.

It was of a delicate oval-shape, with a
rather low forehead, surmounted by soft,
closely-cut hair of a rich, dark brown. His
eyes, which were well-protected by long,
dark eyelashes, were of the darkest shade
of blue, looking almost violet in certain
lights; and they contained such a fund of
laughing humour, sparkling up from their
depths, that it was impossible, on looking
into them, to resist their spell. All who
gazed into them were involuntarily drawn
towards him, for they plainly disclosed the
nobility and honesty of his character. The
profile of his face was moulded on classic
lines, with a long, straight nose of perfect symmetry, a short upper-lip, on which
there was only just a suspicion of coming
manliness, a delicately-curved mouth, the

upper lip of which slightly protruded, and
a well-pointed chin.   His complexion was
of a dark olive, in which the warm colour
flushed and paled continually, giving to
the face a charming air of animation and
attractiveness.   His figure was well pro-
portioned, tall, slim, and active, with a
supple length of limb, and there was a look
of grace about him which the most unob-
servant of beings could not help perceiving.

It was impossible to look upon him without experiencing the feeling that such a
perfect exterior must of necessity contain
a mind and disposition altogether worthy
of it.   Such was the case, and the proof
of it lay in the fact that Frank Grandby
could say with a clear conscience that he
had never made an enemy in his life.
Everyone who had met him liked him.
Attracted in the first instance by the
charm of his person, and afterwards drawn
towards him by the force of the honesty of
his character, all who made his acquaintance had to acknowledge that it was an
acquaintance worth possessing.

But, as has already been hinted, Frank
Grandby himself was incapable of respond-
ing with a similar fervour to those around

him. He hated the shallow pretence of a hollow friendship. He was incapable of appearing affectionate when his heart experienced indifferentism, and he shrank from the selfish life led by most young men, to whom everyone is 'the best chap in the world, 'pon honour,' until he perchance holds some contrary opinion, resulting in a clash of interests. Such a course of proceeding was most repellant to him, and he never felt quite at his ease when in the company of those to whom such an existence was the only one imaginable. Consequently he bore the reputation of being somewhat reserved, and it was even hinted by some that he was inclined to be proud, though neither opinion had any power to eradicate the impression that he was, in spite of all peculiarities, a thoroughly good, honest fellow, possessing character of irresistible weight.

The foregoing description of Grandby's personal appearance hardly tallies with the wearied figure slowly toiling up to Banbury's Hotel. He has been terribly pulled down by the protracted illness which he has lately undergone, and he finds every step he takes a positive exertion to him.

He is in no vein to appreciate the glorious majesty of nature revealing itself on all sides; his one idea is to reach the hotel, and to rest himself.

The gladstone-bag leads the way, and they pass the post-office, and presently leave the main-road, and begin to ascend a path, roughly hewn in the rocks, which is a short cut to Banbury's. Every moment he feels himself growing weaker and weaker, but, in proportion as his strength fails him, his determination not to yield to his growing weakness increases, and he plods steadily on, his face growing paler and paler at every step he takes.

After some minutes of painful exertion, the hotel suddenly confronts him—a large, rambling brick building of picturesque appearance, covered with a net-work of wooden balconies, with a low, sloping roof, surmounted by a multitude of chimneys, emitting faint films of smoke—and the sight of the long-wished-for goal gives him a fictitious strength. He quickens his pace, and finds himself at last on level ground. The effort is past, and, as the thought strikes him, a giddiness overcomes him, and he leans against a tree for support. A sudden faintness steals over him, and his eyes involuntarily close, his breath coming in short gasps, and he feels quite incapable of movement.

He is aroused by a sweet, soft voice, murmuring some gentle words of sympathy.

With a great effort, he masters his weakness, and opens his eyes, and sees standing before him, with an air of shy perplexity, the figure of a young girl, dressed in a soft robe of Indian muslin, trimmed with light-blue ribbons.

He gazes at her in admiration. His senses are still a little bewildered, and at first he is quite dazzled by the loveliness of the *petite* form before him. He eyes her from top to toe, noting every detail of her person, from her wavy, red-gold hair to her tiny little feet peeping from beneath her dress ; and then he somewhat recalls his position, and raises his hat. She gives a graceful little inclination of the head, and her lips part in a half-smile.

'I am so glad that you are better,' she says, softly. 'I was so frightened when I saw you leaning there, with your face as white as a sheet.'

'I must apologise,' he answers, faintly,

'for having made such an exhibition of myself. The truth is, I have just come up from the plains, where I have not been well, and this first experience of hill-climbing has been a little too much for me.'

She smiles again—a roguish, winning smile, which dissipates his sense of embarrassment, causing his lips involuntarily to curl in sympathy. And then there is a pause, and they both stand eyeing each other in amusement. She is the first to break the silence.

'Well, I must be going,' she says. 'You are quite certain that you feel better? Doonga is so intensely proper, you know, that it would never do to be seen talking like this to a perfect stranger.'

He gazes at her for a moment with a glance of open admiration, and then, for the life of him, he cannot help his tongue from blurting out:

'Oh! don't go.'

Immediately he has uttered the words he becomes aware that he has made a very impertinent remark, and he tries to cover his confusion by murmuring inarticulately a lame apology.

A low ripple of laughter issues from

her rosy lips, and she turns round and views him with an arch expression on her face.

'Don't apologise,' she says. 'I can quite understand how awkward you must be feeling at this moment. I should advise you to go and lie down, for you are looking miserably pale, and you are evidently so weak that you have no control whatever over your tongue!'

He tries to stammer some reply. He is very vexed with himself for having been guilty of such an unpardonable *gaucherie*, and a flush of colour sweeps across his pale face. He looks towards her, and she laughs again—she seems to him to be made of smiles and laughter—and then she turns round, and with a graceful little wave of the hand she trips down the path and disappears.

He moves slowly in the direction of the house, skirts the building, and enters the dining-room at the further end, when again a giddiness attacks him, and he has just time to seat himself in an arm-chair, when he faints comfortably away.

As he comes to his senses he finds the manager of the hotel, surrounded by several servants, anxiously regarding him. He rises, with an apology for the trouble that he has given, and asks whether he can have a room. The manager replies that the hotel is full from top to basement, but that he can let him have two small rooms, detached from the house itself, at about one hundred yards' distance. Grandby gladly accepts the offer, and presently he is lying fast asleep in an arm-chair in his own room, in front of a coke-fed stove dreaming of a little laughing figure, clothed in white and blue, seemingly familiar to him, and yet in so vague a manner, as to prevent him from being able to attach to it any distinct personality.

CHAPTER III.

GRANDBY'S INTEREST DEEPENS.

WHEN Grandby wakes up, he finds that it
is nearly four o'clock. He feels very refreshed by his afternoon nap, and he rises
and stretches himself, and then, throwing
off his coat and waistcoat, proceeds to
bathe his face, and wash his hands. Having thoroughly cleansed himself of the dirt
of travelling, and made some necessary
changes in his apparel, he calls a servant,
and orders tea and toast. His tastes are
very simple, and his partiality for this
meal, so dear to feminine minds, has been
the cause for much good-natured sarcasm
on the part of his associates, whose tastes
recoiled before such bare simplicity in the
way of drink.

In a quarter-of-an-hour the little repast
is brought in, and he is soon thoroughly

enjoying it, sitting with the what-not table drawn close up to the stove, for the fresh mountain air is a novel experience to him, and he feels the cold.

He finds himself ravenously hungry, and the quickly-emptied plate is despatched to be refilled. On returning, the hotel servant brings him the visitors' book, and he opens it and slowly looks down the list of names, wondering lazily, for he is now feeling very comfortable, seated in the warmth of the red-hot coke, whether by chance he may come across any familiar to him.

He meets with two or three names he knows more or less well, which recall to him a host of long-forgotten memories, but from the dates affixed to them being of some months past, he rightly concludes that they have long since left the hotel. He is not sorry that he finds himself a total stranger in the place; in his present state of health he feels by no means inclined for the inanities of social life. In fact, he experiences a sense of positive satisfaction at the thought of his being there unknown to all, with the power of choosing his acquaintances at will, should he feel any inclination later on to mix in society. He will in reality be more powerful in his perfect independence than if he were the acknowledged leader of the Doonga social world !

He carries his eye slowly down the list of names, and discovers that there is a distinct dearth of spinsterhood within the precincts of Banbury's Hotel. In fact, amongst the present inmates, he can find only one name bearing the conventional badge of maidenhood.

It is the last entry in the book, and runs as follows :

'COLONEL AND MRS. RENFREW,

MISS DIANA FORSDYKE,'

the two names being bracketed together.

He lights a cigar, and begins to ruminate concerning Miss Diana Forsdyke. He wonders what she is like, and suddenly arrives at the conclusion that she must be very old and scraggy. He can assign no reason for this presentiment as to the lady's personal appearance, but every puff he draws from his cigar convinces him that he is right in his conjecture, and he inwardly determines to make a point of avoiding the elderly damsel.

On re-reading the list of residents staying in the hotel, to his horror he finds that he is the only bachelor amongst them. Every man's name is followed by one or more encumbrances of a similar nomenclature—Colonel and Mrs. Stockton—Major and Mrs. Andrews and children—Mrs. Bird and child—Mrs. Blewitt—Major and Mrs. Lamb, and so on. Banbury's is evidently a family-hotel, and not one patronised by the youthful subaltern, and he begins to think that possibly Loftus may have spoken the truth when he prophesied that he would be bored to death before the first night was over. However, he determines to make the best of things, and he leans back, puffing away at his cigar, in a state of perfect contentment, and closes his eyes in indolent enjoyment,—and immediately there appears before him the vision of a laughing figure, clothed in white and blue.

He leans forward and scans the book with an eager glance. What could he have been thinking of all this time to have totally forgotten the existence of that fairy little form with its crown of gold, which had appeared to him like some ministering angel when he was leaning half-fainting against the tree?

Who is she? What can be her name? That she is unmarried he feels ready to swear to in the highest court of justice. Then if she be unmarried, and if she be residing in Banbury's Hotel, she must— she must be none other than Miss Diana Forsdyke! And to think that he had pictured this lady in his mind as a scraggy old maid! Oh, what a lamentable instance of the unreliability of a vivid imagination!

Miss Diana Forsdyke again becomes the object of his thoughts; but now he takes quite another view of the only spinster in Banbury's Hotel. He entertains now, curiously enough, no sense of disgust, as he contemplates the possibility of the only spinster and the only bachelor being thrown together, and striking up an intimacy with one another. A little social intercourse will perhaps after all, he thinks, not be unbeneficial to him; but he must be careful not to take it to excess! Ah! yes, he must be mindful of his late illness, and never overdo it! There would be no harm, however, in knowing just one or two people—say, for instance, Colonel and

Mrs. Renfrew, and Miss Diana Forsdyke—for, should their combined society prove too exciting to his nerves, it would be a work of no great difficulty for him to gradually drop his intimacy with the over-stimulating factor—say, for instance, with Colonel and Mrs. Renfrew. And then there would be only Miss Diana Forsdyke left, and she, he feels quite certain, would act as a tonic on his shattered nerves. He has not the least doubt in his mind that the society of her charming little person would effect a rapid cure.

And in arriving at this conclusion it must not be thought that Grandby is actuated by any idiotic ideas concerning love and desperate flirtation. He has the sense to know that such luxuries as these are not to be indulged in by one of his tender years. But, being young, he naturally has a craving for young associates, and likewise naturally he has no objection to their being of the opposite sex, possessed of prepossessing personal appearance. So, in the contemplation of his possible future intercourse with Miss Forsdyke, such frivolities as love and kissing take no part whatever. He merely pictures to himself a pleasant friendship, in which he will be able to exchange ideas on all subjects with one of his own age, without entertaining any desire to become more closely intimate, or to relapse into passionate folly. He is very partial to this sort of platonic friendship, in which man and woman can converse freely, and enjoy each other's society, having perfect faith in the fraternal feeling which they bear towards one another, and having no fear that some day a barrier such as love or jealousy may arise between them and mar the harmony of their intercourse.

It is close on six o'clock, when he rises from his chair and proceeds to light the lamp and close the windows. Dusk is descending, and all the hills are bathed in a faint blue mist, and there is a feeling of chilliness in the air. He opens his bag and takes out his leather writing-desk, and sits down and proceeds to write a short letter to Grafton, announcing his safe arrival, and asking him as to what date they may hope to meet again.

As he is writing the address, his heavy luggage, which has come up from the plains in a native cart under charge of his own servant, arrives, and for the next half-

hour he is occupied in the unpacking and
arranging of all his household goods, at the
completion of which uninteresting task he
finds that it is quite time to make his evening toilette.

Owing to his effects being as yet more
or less in disorder, his progress is not so
rapid as it might have been, and he relieves
his feelings by occasionally using some
rather bad language towards his servant,
which need not be recorded here. His
coat is creased, and his shirt-front does not
present an altogether spotless appearance,
and his tie is more refractory than usual,
and he cannot find a pin, and—and he is
fast losing his temper.

In the middle of his difficulties the din-
ner-bell rings. He makes a desperate effort
to overcome the obstinacy of his tie and
partially succeeds, hurriedly brushes his
hair, jerks his arms through his waistcoat,
affixes his watch-chain, and puts on his
coat, and then, with a dissatisfied glance at
his own reflection, he hastily leaves the
house, and hurries towards the hotel.

The residents are already seated at the
dinner-table, and, as he enters, not feeling
so composed as he would have wished, in

spite of his theory regarding the blissful power of independence, two lines of eyes are focussed on his person. There is a slight lull in the conversation, and he feels himself being mentally criticised on all sides, which is rather embarrassing to his affected *sang-froid*. The butler comes quickly to his assistance, and conducts him to a vacant chair. He sits down more rapidly than gracefully, and in a moment his arrival has been forgotten, and conversation resumes its previous swing.

Everyone is busily chatting with his neighbour, and, after a few minutes, Grandby looks round, and proceeds to take stock of his surroundings.

There are about twenty people seated at the table, and, as far as he can judge at first sight, the masculine and feminine elements seem pretty equally divided. He moves his eye up and down the table, scanning each one curiously, and his suspicion as to dearth of youth amongst those residing at Banbury's Hotel is confirmed.

There is nothing very young or attractive to be seen on the opposite side of the table, and, consequently, there is no Miss Diana Forsdyke. This is a disappointment, and he leans back, under the pretence of addressing a servant, and rapidly casts his eye down his own side. He meets with another disappointment, for his own contingent is even more elderly than the opposing force, and there is no one resembling in the least particular the little figure clothed in white and blue.

He experiences something akin to a sense of injury against the sympathetic little stranger for being absent, and he is about to mutter to himself a sentiment of doubtful consonance when the door is thrown open, and a pallid lady, wrapped in a grey woollen shawl, carrying an air-cushion in her hand, enters, followed by the object of his thoughts—a stout, military-looking man, with grey hair and grizzled face, bringing up the rear. There are three vacant chairs, some way down the table, on the opposite side to where Grandby is sitting, and the three late arrivals walk towards them. The pallid lady then hands the air-cushion to Miss Forsdyke, who meekly places it on the chair, and they sit down, the young lady in the middle.

Now that his little acquaintance has actually appeared, Grandby, instead of experiencing a sense of pleasure, is covered with confusion. He fancies that he must be blushing furiously his cheeks seem so hot, and he studiously avoids looking towards the new arrivals, quite at a loss as to what line of conduct he should adopt.

Shall he look towards her, and bow, in virtue of their previous meeting, or shall he steadily ignore her presence? Which is the right thing for him to do? In such a position as this, what does social etiquette require of him?

He has not, certainly, been introduced to the young lady formally; but then, all the same, they have made each other's acquaintance, and, somehow, he does not seem to regard her in the light of a perfect stranger. On the contrary, he feels that he has known her all his life. He fancies that there must be some subtle bond of sympathy existing between them; in no other way can he account for the extraordinary interest which he has conceived for her in so short a time. Possibly, he thinks, *she* may have experienced the same feeling towards him, and probably at this very moment she is looking towards him, wondering why he does not acknowledge

their acquaintance. This consideration decides him, so he suddenly glances towards
her and discovers, to his mortification, that
she is apparently totally unconscious of his
presence.

With her head bent over her plate, she
is toying listlessly with her soup, without
making a pretence to appetite, whilst across
her charming little face is spread an air
of melancholy, which takes him completely
by surprise; for, from his first glimpse of
her that morning, he had concluded that
she was ever in a state of rippling laughter.
But, as he now sees her, her face is so
depressed, that it looks incapable of displaying merriment. He vainly tries to account to himself for such a decided change
in her appearance, but his imagination is
not equal to the task, so he turns his eyes
towards the pallid lady sitting on her left,
and proceeds to take stock of her person.

She is very thin and angular, with a
moist appearance about the eyes, the lids
of which are slightly swollen and of a
purple hue, and she seems so limp that
he half expects to see her fall suddenly
forward, with her face upon her plate.
Her hair, which is of a faded brown, is

bound very plainly across her forehead, and is surmounted by a cap of some black material, and there is a peevish look about her mouth, which does not prepossess him in her favour. Attired in a dress of musty black, totally devoid of trimming, her whole appearance plainly denotes a life of martyrdom, in so far, that he feels it would not surprise him in the least to find a placard attached to her back bearing the words : ' Oh ! look at me, and pity me, for I am the most long-suffering and miserable of women.'

Every other moment she is seized with a spasmodic shiver, and she draws her woollen scarf tightly across her chest, looking over her shoulder with an injured expression, to assure herself that the door is shut ; and, as Grandby studies her person, the thought strikes him that her whims and fancies may possibly have something to do with Miss Forsdyke's depression of spirits. That the lady *is* whimsical and fanciful, he has no doubt—he perceives it in her every gesture—and a feeling of pity arises within him for the young girl's lot. If it be her fate to have to attend to the wants of this elderly invalid, her life must indeed be hard and irksome. Wondering vaguely as to the relationship that they bear towards one another, he turns his eye to the right, and proceeds to inspect the other flank of the fair Diana.

He sees a very stout man, with a large mouth and thick lips, gobbling up his food with an eager voracity approaching to indecency. It is a very coarse face, with bristling grey hair, and a profusion of deep furrows across the forehead, with two little narrow eyes, surmounted by thick, iron-grey eyebrows, with full, bloated cheeks, a nondescript, blotched nose, and a double chin. There is a marked look of greediness depicted on his surly countenance, and Grandby turns away from the contemplation of it with a feeling of disgust. If this gentleman be Diana's guardian for the time being, he can well understand her present depression of spirits. His pity for her increases. How truly sad must be the young girl's life, if it be her fate to pass her days with these two unsympathetic-looking individuals? A hope arises in his heart that he may become intimate with her, and by his influence may be able to brighten her present sombre existence.

The estimate of their respective characters which he has deduced from their external appearances runs as follows: the military old man is the personification of vulgarity and gluttony combined—the elderly lady of the pallid countenance is a snivelling, hypochondriacal, whimsical old idiot—and Miss Forsdyke, sitting meekly between the two, is an angel of purity, innocence, and grace.

This last-named young lady is still keeping her eyes bent upon the table, as though she took no interest whatever in her surroundings. Evidently she is feeling no magnetic attraction drawing her involuntarily towards him. At which discovery he is more than disappointed, for one of his favourite theories is, that every human being is possessed of a certain magnetic fluid permeating his body, which is either attracted to or repulsed from the corresponding fluids of other bodies, according to whether they be of a similar or dissimilar nature, thus controlling the human heart in its likes and dislikes.

Suddenly the pallid lady speaks. Drawing her shawl around her with a spasmodic

E 2

shiver, she addresses her husband in a peevish tone.

'Erasmus,' she says, 'are you quite sure the door is shut?'

'Eh! what d'ye say?' replies her husband, indifferently glancing towards her, with his mouth full.

With a marked sense of injury in her tones, the lady repeats her question.

Her husband turns his head and looks towards the door.

'Yes—the door is shut, my dear,' he says, and he resumes his eating.

She gives a little affected shrug with her shoulders, expressive of discomfort, and turns towards her companion.

'Diana,' she says, sharply, 'why don't you say something? It is so very inconsiderate of you not to make some attempt to amuse me, considering the wretched state of my health. You can be lively enough if you like—no one knows *that* better than I do.'

'Dear aunt, please don't be angry with me,'—the words come out so soft and humbly—'I am not feeling very well tonight—my head is aching.'

'That is because you would go to that

tennis-party this afternoon. It was very, very weak of me to conduct you there. Such excitement I consider quite unnecessary for young girls. In *my* day working in Berlin wool was in vogue, and *we* were quite contented to spend the day at that pleasant and instructive occupation. But now all is different. What was good enough for us is not good enough for you, of—course!' and she points her speech with a little sarcastic sniff.

'Indeed, aunt, you are mistaken,' is the low response. 'I should like to learn how to work in Berlin wools, if you would only be so kind as to teach me.'

'Goodness gracious, Diana, what a preposterous notion! How can you be so inconsiderate? The idea of me, with my wretched health, attempting to instruct you in that graceful accomplishment! From what I know of you, you would take weeks to learn a stitch. No, Diana, a girl who has an objectionable hankering after tennis-parties, is not the pupil for me. What with my neuralgic pains and other ailments, the effort would drive me into the grave. You complain of having a headache to-night. I have had a headache for the last five-and-twenty years, without five minutes' respite,—and yet I have never been heard to complain! You should display more fortitude, Diana, or you are no true niece of mine. The Forsdykes have always been noted for their courage!'

Not a word of this little conversation escapes the ears of Grandby. He has conceived such a powerful interest in the beautiful creature sitting opposite to him, that perhaps he strains his sense of hearing somewhat beyond the borders of good taste; but even had he acted otherwise, and turned his attention towards another quarter, he could not have prevented himself from hearing every syllable uttered, for Mrs. Renfrew—such was the pallid lady's name—makes no effort to lower her voice, in a way suggestive of her conversation being of a confidential nature. She speaks in a thin, piping voice, which travels half-way down the table, as though oblivious to the fact that she is surrounded by a score or so of strangers. In fact, it seems to Grandby, who has already conceived a strong prejudice against her, that she intentionally raises her voice, so as to

allow those around her to fully comprehend that her life is a burden to her,
and that her disposition is remarkable for
the truly angelic patience with which she
bears her sufferings.

Grandby has quite made up his mind by
this time as to the line of action that he
will adopt when Miss Forsdyke chances to
glance his way. He will smile towards
her a look of kindly sympathy, showing
her how thoroughly aware he is of the
sadness of her lot. There is no sense of
embarrassment now in his mind as he
contemplates her look of recognition. He
feels as bold as brass, and determines like
some knight-errant of old to succour the
lovely damsel, in spite of the two dragons
guarding her on either side. So he keeps
his eye steadily fixed on the trio, in expectation of the coming glance.

The colonel is eating as though his very
life depended on his consuming a certain
amount of food in a certain time, and Mrs.
Renfrew is allowing her eyes to wander
listlessly round the table.

She pauses as they alight on Grandby's
classic face, and gives him a steady stare,
which he unflinchingly returns. Then she

half closes her eyes and bends her head
a little to one side, and gazes at him as
though she were critically examining some
chef-d'œuvre in statuary.

'Diana,' she says, in the same high-
pitched voice, which can be heard by
everyone surrounding her, 'who is that
new arrival? His face strongly reminds
me of a statue I took a great fancy to in
the Louvre some years ago.'

Grandby feels the hot blood rushing to
his face as he listens to this criticism on
his personal appearance, but he does not
waver in his glance. He feels that the
long-expected moment has arrived, and
that Miss Forsdyke will look towards him
at last; so he summons up his most pleasing cast of countenance to receive her
glance of recognition.

In answer to her aunt, Miss Forsdyke
looks immediately in the opposite direction
to where he is sitting.

'Which one, aunt?' she says. 'I see no
new arrival.'

'How very provoking you are, Diana!'
says Mrs. Renfrew, peevishly. 'If I want
you to look one way, it is a moral certainty that you will look the other. Do

be more considerate, and try to remember
that the least exertion I make causes me
much extra suffering. I refer to that
young man, sitting between Mrs. Lamb
and Mrs. Stockton, across the table.'

The moment has arrived. He sees Miss
Forsdyke slowly turn her head in his direction and look towards him, but the ready
smile of sympathy which he has prepared
for her freezes on his lips, for she looks at
him with an air of indifferent curiosity,
without a trace of recognition in her face.

' I really do not know, aunt,' she answers,
mildly. ' I suppose that he is a new arrival, for I have never noticed him before.'

' Of course he is a new arrival,' snaps
her aunt, viewing him still in the light of
an inanimate work of art. ' What is the
good of telling me that? You really have
a very annoying manner. If I ever ask
you for information on any point, you are
certain to tell me something which I knew
before you were born. Kindly have a
little more consideration for the wretched
state of my nerves,' and she shivers per-
ceptibly, and relapses into moody silence.

Grandby is astounded. The look of
perfect indifference which she has cast

upon him has taken him so completely by surprise that for some moments he stares towards her in blank amazement. But she does not bestow on him a second glance; she lowers her eyes upon the table-cloth, with an expression of meek humility on her face.

No person's *amour-propre* is proof against the cut direct. There is something so stinging, so deeply humiliating in the fact of one's person being totally ignored that it is impossible for one's vanity to rise superior to the slight unwounded. However strong-minded one may be, and whatever may be the circumstances of the case, a manifestation of contempt such as this always leaves behind it a trace of its subtle poison, which possibly may heal itself in course of time, but which as a rule rankles into a festering sore.

And so it is with Grandby now. Though their acquaintance is of a most informal character, still he feels distinctly hurt at her behaviour. He has not expected that she would nod to him familiarly across the table—the brief conversation that they have held that morning did not warrant such a free-and-easy proceeding on her part—but he certainly thinks, in common justice to himself, that she should have made some sign of recognition, if only a sudden twinkle of the eye. It seems to him that she has been intentionally rude to him, but he determines not to give her the gratification of noting his discomfiture; the stony glance which she has levelled at him has quite hardened his heart towards her. So, affecting a bold front, suggestive of the presence of Miss Diana Forsdyke on this earth being a matter of the supremest indifference to him, he casts towards her a glance of perfect unconcern.

She looks at him from under her eye-lids, and a sudden gleam of light flashes across her eyes; for an instant the sus-picion of a smile hovers about the corners of her mouth, and then again her face resumes its calm expression of humility. She has recognised him!—she has smiled at him covertly too, as though she were afraid of being seen! What mystery is this?

All angry feeling towards her vanishes in a moment, and his sense of interest in her being revives a hundred-fold. What is the reason of her conduct? Why should she be afraid to openly recognise him at a public dinner-table? How is it that she has changed in the short space of six hours from a laughing fairy-sprite to this depressed personification of meekness and humility?

He can arrive at no satisfactory solution of the mystery. He is filled with doubts and suspicions. A yearning comes across him to know more about the girl, and he determines to seize on the first opportunity which presents itself to renew their brief acquaintance. That she is unhappy he feels convinced, and his honest young heart overflows with an infinite compassion for her lot, and the idea of his possibly being able to shed brightness on her existence returns to him with redoubled force.

CHAPTER IV.

' SOMETIMES LADIES HIT EXCEEDING HARD.'

THE dinner progresses slowly, one course
succeeding another in endless monotony,
and Grandby, whose appetite at present is
not of the best, yawns audibly. He is beginning to feel intensely bored with his
own society, and a desire to hear his own
voice asserts itself within him. So he
glances cautiously on either side of him, in
order to form some idea as to his probable
reception, should he be so bold as to address one or other of the company.

He is by no means prepossessed by what
he sees. The two ladies present a striking
contrast to one another, and for the moment he can almost imagine that he has
been suddenly transplanted into the middle
of a travelling-show, with the fat woman
on his right, and the walking skeleton on

his left. From their general style and
mode of dress, it is evident that they both
affect a sprightly manner, and there seems
to be a rivalry existent between the two
as to which of them shall, within the limits
of decency, wear the least amount of
clothes. Anyhow, there is to be seen on
the one side a great display of flesh, and
on the other of skin and bone, and Grandby finds himself gravely considering the
question as to which of his two fair companions is the least unappetising.

'What a pity it is,' he thinks to himself,
'that they cannot be shaken up together
in a tub, and then equally divided. They
might then possibly be two very fine women.'

The lady of the flesh—Mrs. Stockton by
name—is dressed in a full costume of rich
brown-silk, with a massive diamond star
of suspicious brilliancy resting upon her
overflowing bosom; her hair is short and
curly, and is bound with a velvet ribbon,
which, it is whispered, is not so much for
effect as to make certain of the short wavy
locks remaining on her head, popularly
supposed, when unassisted by Art, to resemble the polished surface of a billiard-
ball. But, in the cursory glance which

Grandby takes of her person, he is not able to take note of such minute details as these; he merely sees a very fat face, with heavy overhanging eyebrows, a prominent nose, and long upper-lip, decorated with more than a suspicion of moustache, full red lips, and a well-developed chin, the whole overspread with an expression of latent malignancy, diabolical in its intensity.

The lady of the skin-and-bone—Mrs. Lamb by name—looks as if she had been lately subjected to a thorough washing, wrung-out, dried, and bleached, and her faden appearance is rendered still more bilious by the colour of her dress, which is of a light-blue silk, trimmed with imitation lace. Her pale yellow hair is worn in a little knot on the top of her head, on one side of which is affixed with coquettish carelessness a *gloire-de-Dijon* rose. Her poor, pinched face seems to be composed solely of nose, chin, and cheek-bones, and on closer investigation he discovers that she possesses a partiality for freckles, and he feels a species of thankfulness that she has had the good taste to encase her long lean arms in white lace mittens.

Having completed his examination on

either side, his sudden desire for conversation leaves him, and he resolves to maintain a rigid silence. He glances once more across the table, but he has no power to attract the fair Diana's eyes towards his person. She is apparently engaged in an exhaustive study of the pattern of the damask table-cloth, and she seems to be totally uninfluenced by his close proximity. Mrs. Renfrew is still viewing him in the light of a work of art, with her head on one side, as though she were considering the advisability of effecting a purchase, and he feels so incensed towards her that he hastily turns away, for fear of addressing her as to her extraordinary behaviour.

Suddenly Mrs. Stockton bends forward and addresses Mrs. Lamb.

'Good-evening, Mrs. Lamb,' she says, in a thick, oily voice; 'I trust that you find your hip more easy to-night.'

'Thank you, Mrs. Stockton,' replies Mrs. Lamb, icily, as though to intimate that she objects to having the joints of her body openly discussed at a public dinner-table. 'My *sciatica* is much better this evening; I have been very little troubled with the complaint to-day.'

'I am so glad to hear you say so,' re-joins Mrs. Stockton. 'It would have been so very annoying had you found yourself unable to go to the dance to-morrow night.'

'Yes, it would have been a thousand pities, especially as my card is already nearly full,' she answers, modestly, vainly attempting to raise a blush to her sallow cheeks.

'Really!' says Mrs. Stockton, as though surprised at the announcement. 'That is very nice for you, I am sure. Though, for my own part, I disapprove of the prac-tice of promising dances before the night has arrived. It seems so unfair on the majority of the men.'

'I cannot agree with you in that par-ticular, Mrs. Stockton. I think that a lady has a right to choose her own partners, and, if she allows herself to enter the room with a blank card, it is almost certain that she will find herself engaged to dance with those whom she would rather avoid.'

'That may be your experience, Mrs. Lamb, but it certainly is not mine. You should have tact to extricate yourself from such an unpleasant position. It is very easily done. You can say that you are tired, and do not mean to dance, or you can assert that your card is already full.'

'I am sure that I am very much obliged to you for your kind advice,' returns Mrs. Lamb, with an ominous twitching of her thin lips. 'But I am sorry to have to say that I hope I shall never take advantage of it. I have been brought up to understand that such deceit on the part of a lady is neither creditable nor well-bred.'

'Oh! really,' says Mrs. Stockton, with the faintest sarcasm. 'I am sure I beg your pardon for having attempted to interfere with your ideas of right and wrong. I am really proud to possess the acquaintance of a lady who never swerves in the slightest degree from the path of virtue. A love of right is an admirable trait in an individual's character, but in order to obtain my full respect there should be consistency in every action;' and she gives a little grunt of approval, as though immensely pleased at her own remark.

'May I ask,' says Mrs. Lamb, leaning forward, very pale, and speaking with quite unnecessary politeness, 'whether you are speaking generally, or whether you are alluding to any special case? From the tenor of your remarks, I should conclude that you are making a personal reference to me. If such be the case, allow me to tell you that your observations are un-called-for and offensive.'

'My dear Mrs. Lamb, what a most extra-ordinary idea,' exclaims Mrs. Stockton, with a malicious smile overspreading her heavy countenance. 'Nothing was further from my thoughts, I can assure you. You will excuse me stating that your vehemence is unnecessary, and quite unpardonable. You should really be more careful in your tone of address, and not speak so thoughtlessly. I need not remind *you*, Mrs. Lamb, who pride yourself so vastly on your knowledge of Continental life, that there is a French proverb, the truth of which is generally admitted, that "*qui s'excuse s'accuse.*"'

An angry flush lightens up Mrs. Lamb's pallid countenance.

'Your pronunciation of the French lan-guage, Mrs. Stockton,' she retorts, quickly, 'could hardly be called Parisian, even by your best of friends. But, from my inti-mate knowledge of the language in ques-tion, I fancy that I know to which proverb you are referring. At the same time, I may state that it is, in my opinion, a sign of great vulgarity to parade a smattering of a foreign tongue in a way to impress one's audience that one is a master of the language. Take my advice, Mrs. Stockton, and keep to your native tongue. It is quite adequate for the expression of any ideas which *your* intellect may form, and you will find it sufficiently rich in ancient adages to do away with the necessity of borrowing from the Continent. To illustrate this remark, I need only mention "That those who live in glass houses should not throw stones." '

The two ladies, in the heat of their argument, have apparently quite lost sight of the immediate presence of Frank Grandby. Conscious of his position becoming more and more uncomfortable every moment, he gives a little cough to recall his proximity to their minds, but without effect ; so he leans forward, and affects to study the *menu,* thereby hoping to raise an effectual barrier between the fair opponents. But in this also he is disappointed. Mrs. Stockton merely changes her position, and leans back with her hand upon his chair.

'Pray excuse my mentioning, Mrs. Lamb,'

she says, with dangerous suavity, 'that personalities, instead of being witty, as you presumably consider them to be, are merely vulgarities of the most disgusting type. I am surprised that I should have to mention such a well-known fact to a lady of *your* age.'

'You will kindly oblige me, Mrs. Stockton, by making no reference to my age,' retorts Mrs. Lamb, with asperity. 'It is quite beyond the point. I may not be so young as I was, but still I am many, many years *your* junior, and I am glad to say that I have not to descend to any deceptions in order to appear presentable.'

'What do you mean?' says the lady of the flesh, flushing hotly.

'I mean just what I say—I have nothing false about me, and I should have no hesitation in swearing the same before any court of justice. No—I thank my God that I can affirm truthfully that every hair on my head is my own, and is fixed firmly by the roots.'

'A truly highly interesting piece of information!' returns Mrs. Stockton, with sarcastic emphasis. 'Perhaps, as you have begun the subject, you will favour

the company with a detailed analysis of
your whole person. This is really most
edifying, but I must confess that I miss
the point.'

'The point is this,' says Mrs. Lamb,
trembling all over with excitement, and
raising her voice to its highest pitch—
'If I were situated in a similarly unfortunate position to that which you are, I
should be too proud to resort to such a
low and disgusting artifice as that of attempting to conceal my defect by the application of a dead woman's hair.'

The dispute has been carried on with
so little regard to their surroundings that
everyone seated at the table has gradually
stopped talking, so as to try to discover
the point of the discussion, so that the
last remark, offered by Mrs. Lamb with
tremendous force, has fallen upon an
almost silent room. Every eye is directed
in amused curiosity towards the two
antagonists, and Grandby feels so embarrassed that he has half a mind to jump up
and leave the room with all possible haste.

His position is really a most delicate
one. The two ladies have now lost their
tempers to such a degree that he half ex-

pects to find them fighting across his body. It is such a novel experience to him that he is quite nonplussed as to what he ought to do.

Ought he to rise, and respectfully beg that the ladies should confine their private disputes to their private rooms, or ought he to attempt the rôle of mediator, and do his best to pacify the combatants? Which would be the better course to adopt? He has not the remotest idea, and he feels positively certain that no reference to any 'Guide to Social Etiquette' would simplify the difficulty. What his heart prompts him to do is to rise and seize them both by the scruffs of the neck, and to bang their heads together with all possible force: but luckily he does not attempt to carry out the notion.

He merely sits still, affecting the deepest interest in the *menu*, and silently wondering what is going to happen next.

And this is what happens next. Mrs. Stockton, with a face purple with indignation, leans straight across him.

'Mrs. Lamb,' she says, slowly, 'you will allow me to inform you that you are an infamous liar.'

It is really difficult to describe accurately what follows on this remark of Mrs. Stockton. For a moment there is a dead silence, and then there breaks forth a murmur of the strongest disapproval from the company in general. Such language as has just been uttered is an outrage against all decency, and the room is filled with a rustle of indignation, in the midst of which Mrs. Lamb suddenly falls back in her chair, and bursts into tears.

'Oh, Charles!' she sobs, turning to her husband. 'Take me away—I cannot stay here to be insulted by that dreadful woman.'

The gallant major pulls his tawny moustache, slowly considering what he had better do, and then he rises and conducts his wife from the room. Mrs. Stockton follows the drooping figure of her rival with her eyes across the room with a malignant smile upon her face, which culminates in a chuckle of delight as the door is closed behind her.

'Hush, my dear—be quiet, my love,' says her husband, with a look of misery on his face, speaking for the first time, and touching her on the arm. 'You must not

really become so excited—it is not good
for you.'

She casts on him a look of fierce contempt, and he quickly retires within himself, looking the most down-trodden and
abject of men. She herself then gives
vent to another prolonged chuckle, and
glances triumphantly round the room.
She finds every face studiously turned
away, at which a grim smile settles on her
heavy face, and she turns her attention to
the tray of delicacies at her side, helping
herself with a lavish hand.

In a moment the contretemps has been,
if not forgotten, put aside, and the conversation begins again with renewed
vivacity. Within the space of ten minutes Major Lamb returns, and Grandby,
who eyes him rather curiously, fancies that
he sees him wink significantly at Colonel
Stockton as he enters. Mrs. Stockton
casts on him one furious glance of hatred,
which has no effect whatever on his admirable composure, and then she turns her
attention again to her pistachio nuts.

In the midst of all this excitement
Grandby has forgotten for the moment the
existence of the fair Diana, but now that

peace is again restored her image rises in his brain, and he quickly looks towards her to find her sitting in exactly the same listless attitude as before, apparently taking no interest whatever in what is going on around her. Even the disgraceful *fracas* which has just taken place on his side of the table has had no power to arouse her from her apathetic reverie. A half-doubt arises in his mind that, perhaps, after all, in spite of her attractive person, she may be only an ordinary schoolgirl miss, incapable of forming one idea or of framing a single sentence beyond 'yes' and 'no.'

But immediately there arises within him the memory of that little fairy form sparkling with fun and laughter which had appeared to him that morning by the tree, and all doubts concerning her intelligence disappear.

No, it is neither shyness nor stupidity that makes her behave in this peculiar manner, of that he feels convinced. It is something else, but what it is he is unable to conceive. But he determines, come what may, to discover the reason of her mysterious conduct as soon as possible, for every moment he finds his interest deepening in her personality.

Mrs. Renfrew is talking in the same high-pitched, piping voice—talking as though she were unaware of the presence of anybody in the room besides herself and her niece Diana.

'I have lived for many years,' she is saying, 'and, owing to my wretched health, the years have not gone by so quickly as they might have done; but I can safely say that, amidst all my varied experiences, I have never witnessed anything so disagreeable and trying to the nerves as the discussion which we have just been compelled to listen to across the table.'

Grandby inwardly groans as he hears her speaking. He foresees another storm impending, and the club, with its listless, languid inmates, rises before him, by force of contrast, as a dream of Elysian happiness.

What, in the name of fortune, could the man have meant who told him that Banbury's Hotel was dull? Dull! Can a pitched battle, with the shells bursting and the cavalry charging, and the shrieks of the wounded and dying rising to heaven, through the glare and smoke, be termed *dull?* Then, if not, why should Banbury's be dubbed with such an inapplicable epithet?

Grandby, young as he is, has had the good fortune to have seen some active service in the latter part of the Afghan campaign; but sitting now, in expectation of the coming strife, he feels that his military experiences go for nothing, and that his mind and courage are alike unable to stand against this Amazonian style of warfare.

'I may say, Diana,' continues Mrs. Renfrew, 'that, although I have been an eye-witness of the scene, still my senses refuse to credit it. I ask myself—can it be possible that such a thing has happened? Have not my eyes and ears deceived me? Or is it really true that I have heard two ladies, sitting at a public table . . .'

'Oh! please, aunt, do not speak so loud,' said Diana, in a distressed voice, looking furtively around her; but she speaks so low that Grandby is unable to hear what she says.

'I have yet to learn, Diana,' answers Mrs. Renfrew, severely—so severely that Grand-

by feels the colour mounting to his face as
he hears her speak—'I have yet to learn
that my manners are open to criticism by
such as you. You will excuse me mentioning, Diana, that you are hardly the person
to whom I look for advice. If what your
father writes concerning you is true, it
would, perhaps, be more advisable on your
part to imitate, instead of attempting to
instruct. Understand me, I am not accus-
ing you—I am by no means endorsing
your father's opinion concerning you. I
merely refer to what he has written, without being biassed one way or the other.
At the same time I may remark that, if a
father's word about his own child is not to
be believed, then the world must be wicked
beyond human conception—in fact, so
wicked that my mind is utterly incapable
of grasping such a sinful state of affairs.'

A sudden fire flashes from Miss Forsdyke's eyes, and he sees her raise her head
haughtily, as though with the intention of
making some quick retort. But in a moment
she has remembered her situation, and she
turns away her head without opening her
lips.

'Now, don't apologise,' continues Mrs.

Renfrew, in the same high-pitched strain. 'You were wrong, and you wish to admit it; but do so silently. My nerves are not able to bear the least excitement. Never be violent in action or speech—it is not lady-like. And that reminds me of the subject on which I was speaking when you chose to interrupt me in such a truly unpleasant manner. I was saying, I remember, that my senses refuse to believe that I have actually heard two ladies, sitting at a public dinner-table, openly reviling each other. It is the most discreditable, most disgraceful . . .'

At this moment Grandby's heart seems to stop still, for his next-door neighbour, who has been watching Mrs. Renfrew during her harangue with a wary eye, leans forward and emits a loud 'Ahem!'

'It is the most discreditable and disgraceful seene,' continues Mrs. Renfrew, imperturbably, 'that I have ever had the misfortune . . .'

Grandby dare not look sideways, but he knows in his heart that the moment of battle has arrived. A great rustling of clothes and clearing of the throat—preparations for the coming fight—strike upon his ear, and then the first shell is thrown by Mrs. Stockton emitting a loud angry grunt. There is no warding off the conflict now. The time for mediation is past and gone, and the battle is imminent, and with a groan he resigns himself despairingly to the unpleasantness of his position.

As the first shell bursts, Mrs. Renfrew pauses in her remark. Though surprised at the desperate proximity of the enemy, she does not lose her presence of mind, but, with the eye of a true general, she grasps the whole situation in a moment. After a short silence, she again attempts to speak.

'Yes, Diana,' she says, slowly and collectedly, 'it is the most discreditable and disgraceful scene that I have ever . . .'

She is interrupted by a second explosion of a more decided character.

'I beg your pardon, madam,' says Mrs. Stockton, leaning forward in a very hot and angry state, and vainly endeavouring to imitate her adversary's composure, 'I beg your pardon, but may I ask to what you are referring?'

Mrs. Renfrew possesses two of the most essential qualities necessary for successful leadership—coolness and determination.

In the very face of the attack she never
wavers. Her demeanour is calm—nay,
placid, inspiring all around her with confidence in her powers. Determined to the
best of her ability to conceal her position,
she makes no sign of counter-attack, but
with praiseworthy perseverance again for
the third time attempts to complete her
sentence.

' Yes, Diana, it was the most discreditable
and disgraceful . . .'

The attacking general, exasperated by
the line of action adopted by the enemy,
advances boldly to the front. She is
determined to force it to expose its position by returning her fire, and to this
effect, without more hesitation, she fires a
salvo into its trenches.

' You will kindly have the good manners
to answer a lady when she addresses you,'
she says, excitedly. ' I ask you whether
your highly offensive remarks are directed
at me or not—and I want an answer.'

Mrs. Renfrew's coolness is really admirable. She never moves a muscle, or shows
by sign or gesture that she is conscious of
the magnitude of the attack. Her face
assumes a plaintive expression, and she

gives her shoulders a piteous little shrug.

'Really, Diana, people *ought* to be more considerate for my nerves,' she says. ' There is nothing so trying to one in my present weak state of health as to have to be continually repeating the same remark. It is really very annoying, for, besides the mental suffering it inflicts, the remark itself loses much of its pungency of character by useless repetition. This is actually the fourth time that I have attempted to say that it was the most discreditable and disgraceful scene . . .'

'Madam, do you hear me?' cries Mrs. Stockton, desperately.

'That I have ever had the misfortune to . . .' continues Mrs. Renfrew, calmly ignoring her adversary.

'Will you answer me or not?' Mrs. Stockton is becoming furious.

'Witness during the whole . . .'

'I will not stand this insolence!'

'The whole of my life,' says Mrs. Renfrew, with a triumphant ring in her voice. 'And now, Erasmus,' addressing her husband, who has been eating his dessert throughout the encounter, supremely indifferent to the danger,—'and now, Erasmus, will you kindly ascertain for me what the lady across the table is wanting. You know my fixed rule, never to speak to anyone without a formal introduction.'

It is a masterly stroke of genius. A wave of amusement sweeps down each side of the table, and Grandby turns away his head to hide a smile.

'Eh! What?' growls the colonel, gruffly, pausing with half a banana on his fork midway between his mouth and the table. 'What was that remark you made?'

'There is a lady, across the table, who, I believe, has a wish to communicate with me. Not having been introduced to her, I am unable to treat with her personally. Will you be so good as to ascertain her business?'

Colonel Renfrew eyes his wife meditatively for a moment, and then he opens his mouth, and inserts the banana, which he leisurely begins to masticate.

Except at the lower end of the room, from which proceed sounds of muffled laughter, there is a dead silence in the room. Miss Forsdyke, with a slight flush on her fair cheeks, is looking demurely on her plate, whilst Mrs. Stockton is fuming and snorting to such an extent that she has assumed an apoplectic hue.

Colonel Renfrew does not move till he has swallowed his banana, and then he turns his head, and glances across the table. He shows none of that coolness which his wife has displayed; for, on meeting Mrs. Stockton's infuriated gaze, his face becomes the colour of a lobster, and he hastily turns away.

' My dear,' he says, 'what applies to you applies to me. Not having the pleasure of her acquaintance, I am equally unable to address the lady in question;' and he stretches out his hand mechanically, and removes another banana from the plate in front of him.

At this diplomatic reply the whole company burst out laughing, in the midst of which the lady at the head of the table gives the signal, and they all rise. The ladies file out one by one, Mrs. Renfrew without a trace of excitement on her face, and the fair Diana looking coyly on the ground.

Mrs. Stockton is the last to go. She rises angrily from her seat, and bends over her husband, and speaks to him in a sharp

G 2

whisper, with great volubility of tongue.

'Hush, my dear,' says the colonel, mildly. 'You really *must* not become so excited, my love—it is not good for you.'

'Keep quiet yourself, *booby !*' she cries, at the top of her voice; and with flushed face, and haughty carriage of the head, she leaves the discomfited man, and takes her departure from the room.

CHAPTER V.

ANOTHER GLIMPSE.

IT is generally supposed that a good,
sound, uninterrupted sleep is proof of a
clear conscience. Certainly Frank Grandby's conscience was as clear and unsullied
as a running crystal stream, but whether
this was the reason of his enjoying a perfect night's rest, or whether it was due to
the extreme weariness of his body, cannot
really be said. The fact remains that he
slept long and placidly, undisturbed by
night-mare horrors.

A confused sense of pleasant, well-known
scenes and faces floats within his brain, and
gradually a half-smile breaks upon his lips.
The morning sun, rising fresh from behind
the dewy hills, peeps in through the open
window and falls upon his face, and Aurora,
perceiving that he is beautifully made,

hovers about his form, pressing warm kisses
on his face and neck. She gazes long and
lovingly on his classic face, and notes the
perfect symmetry of his profile, and then
a longing comes over her to see the colour
of his eyes; and so the amorous jade
casts upon him such a fiery glance that he
feels it through his slumbers, and he opens
his eyes to find the sun pouring in upon
him through the window.

With the morning air blowing in fresh
and cool, he feels so well, both in body
and spirit, that he is unable to remain in
bed; so he jumps out, and proceeds to the
window, and cautiously—for he has no
wish for either Mrs. Stockton or Mrs. Lamb
to see him in his night-dress—looks out.

However, he is quite safe—there is no
disturbing element to be seen. Everything is calm and peaceful, and the sun,
appearing above the tops of the distant
hills, amidst a haze of gold, is quickly
scattering the faint blue mist, thereby dis-
closing all the towering heights and well-
wooded slopes to his wondering eyes.

Leaving the window, he hastily plunges
into his tub, and dresses with all speed.
On such a glorious morning as this, it

seems a positive crime to remain indoors. So he orders a simple breakfast to be brought to his room, and, having despatched it with indecorous haste, he sallies forth, with his thick stick, intent on exploring some of the beauties of the Doonga hill.

The mountain air has braced him up to such an extent, that he already feels a different individual from that weary creature of the day before, and he walks down the hill, gaily swinging his stick in the air. He feels very happy and contented with himself and all things on this particular morning. The charm of the magnificent scenery slowly unveiling itself on all sides under the influence of the rising sun is too strong to be resisted, and his heart beats with a tumultuous sense of gladness, and he feels at peace with all men.

Snatches of operatic melody rise to his lips as he strolls along, and then suddenly his thoughts revert to the disputes which he has witnessed the night before during dinner, and so light-hearted and contented does he feel, that he laughs aloud at the recollection.

He is not a little exercised, though, con-

cerning his future line of action. The
experience of the night before has been as
disagreeable as it has been novel, and, if
it is to be taken as a fair example of the
manners and customs of Banbury's Hotel,
he thinks that perhaps it would be better
for his health and peace of mind if he
were to change his place of abode.

But where is he to go to? That is the
question which puzzles him. Certainly
there are many other hotels in Doonga,
but then probably they are much of a
muchness with regard to the attractions
which they offer to the bachelor subaltern.
Banbury's, he knows to be universally acknowledged the best hotel in Doonga, so
to betake himself to another one would
probably be a case of stepping off the fry-
ing-pan into the fire.

Then there is the club! Twenty-four
hours ago he had shuddered at the very
idea of residing there in his present state
of health; but in the last few hours his
bachelor mind has been somewhat enlight-
ened as to the joys and peacefulness of a
family hotel, and the club does not now
appear to him so horrible in consequence.
However, he determines to do nothing

rashly. He will wait awhile, and watch the progress of affairs. At any rate, he can change his position at the dinner-table; at a distance the fights may not appear so terrible. And if the worst comes to the worst—if, in fact, the whole table should throw themselves heart and soul into the contest—then he will take refuge in his little hut, and eat his meals in peaceful solitude.

Passing the post-office and the little church, he turns on to the Mall, and proceeds along the road, and arrives at the club, lying down below him. But he does not stop; he feels a new sense of life permeating his veins, and he walks along at a brisk pace, gazing across, with a keen appreciation of the beautiful, at the opposite range of hills. From this point the road commences to slightly incline upwards, and he soon becomes conscious of the fact, for in a moment or two his breath begins to fail him, and his pace visibly slackens. However, he is nothing daunted. He is in such buoyant spirits at finding himself once more breathing cool, fresh air that he laughs softly to himself at his increasing weakness as he plods steadily along the winding road.

On his left rises an almost perpendicular wall of rock and foliage, for the road has been blasted out of the hill-side; but on his right a panorama of Nature's greatest majesty is unrolled before his bewildered eyes. The hill is looking very lovely in the morning light, with its masses of dark green foliage, speckled here and there with little villas, shining in the soft sunlight, and he pauses for several moments, gazing back at the brilliant scene. A giant ravine separates him from the opposite range of hills, and far down in its peaceful depths he can discern the running mountain stream, decked on either side with native huts, surrounded by their little plots of cultivated land. The reality of the Himalayas has exceeded his most sanguine anticipations, and his heart grows soft and tender in the contemplation of the majesty of their creation. His thoughts revert to Dhobipur, with its sickening glare and heat, its fierce, pitiless, brassy sun, its dust and discomforts, and long, long weary day, and now all these seem to him as some vague nightmare of the past. And yet less than forty-eight hours have elapsed since he was in their midst.

After a short time he continues his walk up the gradual incline, and, refusing to yield to his increasing weakness, he does not rest until he has reached the summit of Garam Point. Here he throws himself down upon the grass, thankful to ease his limbs, and he gazes down in silence on the glorious landscape stretched before him. Woods, mountain peaks, boulders of massive proportions and long stretches of grass and corn, all enveloped in a faint blue mist, parade themselves before him, and he takes them all in greedily, feasting his eyes in rapture on the magnificent display. Range upon range tower above one another as far as the eye can reach, and every moment fresh beauties are revealed by the gradually dispersing mist.

Far in the distance can be obtained a glimpse of the plains. It is in the vicinity of Garamabad, and there is a thick haze overhanging it. There, he knows, the temperature is standing over 100° in the verandah, and he sighs with a divine sense of thankfulness that he has had the good-fortune to escape from its horrors for a period. The gurgling sound of a little brook strikes upon his ear, and he listens with a dreamy sense of satisfaction to it finding its way step by step from the summit to the base, there to join the lukewarm stream which can just be discerned occasionally far away down in the plains. A subtle fragrance rises from the flowers scattered round him in wild profusion, and a feeling of great contentment overcomes him as he lies there, attempting to realise the wondrous change in his existence.

'There is still something to live for,' he murmurs to himself. 'A month ago I was actually longing to die, and *now*—how differently I feel! Were I to die now, it would not be from weariness of life, but from excess of happiness.'

A faint breeze sweeps up the hill, and gently stirs the yellow balsam, rustling the leaves and flowers together with a sound refreshing to the ear; and Grandby relapses into a deep reverie. He thinks of his home, with its gentle mistress, whom he has never known to have addressed to him one unkind word since he left her knee, and he tries to picture in his mind her occupation at that moment; and then his thoughts revert to Grafton, and he murmurs softly to himself,

'Ah, my dear old friend, I would lay down my life to please you!'

Within a day or two he expects to hear from him, stating the probable date of his arrival, and he imagines to himself the perfect happiness which they will enjoy living together in this glorious place. His heart is as yet too young to have ever had engraven on it a woman's name in letters which could not have been effaced without a moment's trouble, but in its place, in letters so firmly cut that the lapse of ages could not obliterate them, is to be found the name of 'George Grafton.' To him he was loyal in every thought and action ; never for one moment had that grave, earnest friend been removed from the high pedestal to which he had been raised in the old school-days.

He is roused from his reverie by the noise of voices in the distance, and he leans over on his elbow and glances up the road, and sees a dandy, with a lady sitting within it, approaching. By her side, with her hand resting on the woodwork, is walking a young lady, whom he immediately recognises. It is Miss Diana Forsdyke, and directly the lady in the dandy speaks he has no longer doubt as to her personality. When once heard, it was not easy to forget the high-pitched piping voice of Mrs. Renfrew.

His own position is partially concealed by the long yellow balsam amidst which he has thrown himself, and he turns over and rests his chin in his hands, and takes a criticising survey of the approaching ladies. There is no doubt that he does feel a most unaccountable interest in this young lady; there is an air of mystery about her being which puzzles him, and piques his curiosity.

She is dressed very plainly, but very neatly, with a cloud of some soft material wound carelessly round her neck, and he notices that she is looking superbly lovely, with her delicate fair skin flushed with healthy exercise. Mrs. Renfrew is talking very volubly, and he can hear distinctly what she is saying when she is still some fifty yards away. These are the first words which strike his ear:

'No, Diana, it is quite out of the question. I wonder really how you *can* be so inconsiderate! The idea of my going out to a dance, and sitting up till midnight! It would be the death of me.'

And then Miss Forsdyke says something which he does not hear.

'What a notion!' is the reply, in a peevish tone of voice. 'Only for an hour, indeed! You wish me to dress and turn out after dinner, and to go down to the club merely to watch you dance for an hour? It is really very selfish of you to suggest such a thing.'

'I only made the suggestion, aunt,' replies Miss Forsdyke, humbly, 'thinking that it might be agreeable to you. One hour's amusement would not be over-exciting to your nerves, and I think it would do you good. You would be sure to enjoy yourself, sitting surrounded by your friends. You know how popular you are.'

Oh! Diana, Diana, is this truth, or merely soothing flattery? Is your tongue obeying the dictates of your conscience when you speak, or are you applying butter with a lavish hand, in order to remove all friction from the rusty machinery of Mrs. Renfrew's mind? Grandby, smiling to himself, without hesitation decides in favour of the latter.

Mrs. Renfrew answers her niece in a rather mollified tone of voice.

' Yes, Diana—I am popular,' she says, complacently, '*universally* popular, I may say, I think, without being deemed conceited. But I value my health far more than my popularity, and, if the worst comes to the worst, I must sacrifice the latter to the former.'

' Ah! *that* will never come to pass, dear aunt,' cries Miss Forsdyke, eagerly. 'Do what you may, you will always command the same love and admiration from those around you, as you do now.'

'You are a very good girl,' says Mrs. Renfrew, in tones still sweeter than before. 'There may be truth in what you say. I never courted popularity, and yet I am popular—so perhaps there is a *je ne sais quoi* about me which compels confidence and affection.'

'There is, aunt, there is!' cries Miss Diana, applying the butter in great lumps. 'No one can see you without loving you. How *I* shall ever be able to repay you for your great kindness to me, I do not know. Every moment which passes places me deeper in your debt.'

They are passing him now, and he makes no effort to conceal himself; but the two ladies are so intent upon their conversation that they do not seem to see him. The dandy sails past him to the tune of shuffling feet, and presently Miss Forsdyke drops her handkerchief, and bends down to pick it up. In doing so, she looks straight towards him, and smiles the same roguish smile that she has bestowed upon him at the time of their first meeting. But, before he can make a movement in response, she holds her finger up to her mouth, enjoining him to silence, and then she turns away and re-joins the dandy.

He half-imagines that he has been dreaming. What a charming smile it was! Her eyes seemed to thrill through and through him with a rush of fire.

What does it all mean? Why should she be so afraid to confess that he is known to her? His mind is filled with questioning concerning the lovely vision, and he fully determines to make her acquaintance formally as soon as possible. He feels morally convinced that there is existent between them a bond of sympathy which cannot be ignored.

The two ladies have now proceeded some fifty yards down the hill. Mrs. Renfrew's voice floats towards him.

' I am very sorry, Diana, for your sake,' she says, ' but it is really quite out of the question. We will spend a quiet little evening together, and I must do my best to make you forget the club and its inmates by making myself especially agreeable.'

What Miss Forsdyke's answer is he does not hear, but it is evidently of an oleaginous character; for Mrs. Renfrew immediately leans forward, and says, with the greatest effusion,

' Oh, you sweet girl! You must kiss me directly we get in—now, don't forget !' and then a turn in the road hides them from his sight.

CHAPTER VI.

A PESSIMIST OF THE NINETEENTH CENTURY.

FRANK GRANDBY lies for fully half-an-hour amidst the yellow balsam with his thoughts centred on the personality of Miss Diana Forsdyke. His young and tender heart feels a strange sympathy towards her. There is a something in the startling loveliness of her face which is peculiarly attractive to him, and he is unable to drive her laughing figure from his mind; for, in all his mental visions of her person, she is always depicted as she first appeared to him—smiling and childlike, and not as he has seen her since—demure and grave.

It is this strange change in her demeanour which puzzles him. Had she appeared to him always in the same laughing humour, probably he would not have bestowed on her a second thought. But, as

H 2

it is, he cannot prevent himself from attempting to picture in his mind the probable cause of her depression in public. That she is not sad by nature, he feels assured. Then why does she adopt this melancholy *rôle* when in the presence of her relatives? The only solution to the problem is that her aunt and uncle are unkind to her, and that she is actually afraid to laugh and talk and be generally merry when they are present.

His honest young heart swells with indignation as he arrives at this conclusion, and he rises from the ground feeling an infinite pity towards the young girl whose lot appears so hard.

Looking at his watch, he finds that it is half-past eleven, so he begins to saunter homeward, inwardly anathematising every aunt and uncle in existence, but reserving a special clause for Colonel and Mrs. Renfrew.

Arriving at the club, he pauses a moment, and then decides to go down and see whether there are any of his acquaintances to be seen. An air of desolation overhangs the building. The verandahs are deserted, the arm-chairs and sofas are unoccupied, the papers lie untouched—not a single human creature meets his eye.

Lost in wonder, he enters the building, and finds the whole place upside down. The corridor is almost impassable from the masses of furniture—chairs, tables, sofas, carpets, and divers ornamental cabinets—which are piled up in every conceivable direction. From within, the sound of much hammering, accompanied by violent altercations in the native tongue, strikes upon his ear. He opens a door and looks in, discovering a crowd of natives dispersed about a large empty room, and then he remembers it is the day of the dance, and he laughs to himself at the chaotic aspect which the house presents in consequence.

He wonders where the residents of the club can be! It seems strange on this particular morning, when there must be so much to do, that there should not be a single individual to be seen. Possibly they may be engaged on special duties which have called them away for the moment, he thinks to himself, as he stands half-doubtful what to do. However, he decides before going to see whether Loftus is in his room, so, having ascertained the number, he walks down the flight of steps and enters the verandah of the basement.

Number eight! The door is closed, and there is an air of peaceful quiet about the room suggestive of its being untenanted for the time being. No!—there is not much doubt that Loftus is out, engaged upon some pressing business connected with the dance. So Grandby determines to leave his card, and return to Banbury's for lunch. He opens the door and enters, and immediately a very strong oath falls upon his ear.

There is a blazing fire burning in the grate, and the temperature of the room is distinctly high. The atmosphere is thick and cloudy, and redolent of tobacco smoke, and a suspicious smell of spirits excites his olfactory nerves. In one corner of the room can be discerned a bed, and there in the bed, with head just appearing above the clothes, is the figure of Vernon Loftus, lying with eyes closed, cigar in mouth, and whisky-and-soda clasped tenaciously in the right hand.

Grandby shuts the door behind him, and gazes with amused astonishment at the prostrate form before him. A look of

utter weariness is imprinted on his by no
means unpleasant-looking face, and he is
pulling laboriously at his cigar as though
each puff involved an effort of no mean
order. Prefaced by a highly-embellished
oath, a low growl issues from his lips,

'Call me at one o'clock, you darned old
fool!'

At this Grandby is unable to restrain
himself, and he bursts out laughing.

'Great heavens!' cries Loftus, jumping
up. 'What a delightful surprise! Is that
really you, old chap? I thought it was
the nigger come to wake me. Sit down,
will you, and have a peg?'

Grandby laughingly declines.

'Oh! but you *must* have a peg. Now,
come, Grandby, don't be a damned cad!'

'Well, if you put it in that way, I suppose I must,' returns Grandby, feeling, in
spite of himself, rather vexed.

'Of course you must! Never refuse a
peg when it is offered to you, and never
fail to offer one when you have the chance.
That's the maxim I follow, and, by gad,
sir, you couldn't have a better one.'

Grandby helps himself from the decanter,
and the servant is called to open the soda-

water; then a cigar is pressed upon him, and Loftus languishly murmurs his approval of the proceeding, garnishing his speech with an oath of peculiarly high flavour.

'You appear to be taking a European morning with a vengeance,' remarks Grandby, smiling.

'Ya-as!' says Loftus, with a prolonged yawn. 'Life is really very wearisome. The wonder to me is how we manage to exist at all. I tell you what it is, Grandby,' he adds, somewhat brightening up, 'this world's creation is a very inferior piece of work.'

Having uttered this sentiment, he falls back again upon the pillow, and lazily applies his glass to his lips, and chokes in consequence.

'There are so many faulty arrangements in it,' he continues, after he has recovered from his fit of coughing, 'that it is absurd to attempt to specify anything in particular. There is no change, no variety, always the same wearisome, monotonous routine. One can tell to a moment, with the help of an almanac, the exact time the sun will rise and set—and they are always right—there is no chance of any excitement in *that* direction. It never goes wrong or gets out of order. It is such an inconsiderate mode of conduct, too,' he continues, in an aggrieved tone. 'It was all very well, perhaps, when the world was first made and the inhabitants were savage-like and illiterate. But, in these days of culture and fine art, we have a right to expect something different. How much better it would be now, supposing that once a week —say Sunday—the sun did not rise till midday.'

'What on earth for?' cries Grandby, smiling.

'To give one a good night's rest, of course! Our bodies are, unfortunately, made on such a primitive design that they need constant rest to keep them in health. And, how can one obtain rest, if the sun always rises early in the morning?'

'By going to bed early, I should say,' smiles Grandby.

'My dear Grandby, what an extraordinary idea! Where the deuce have you picked up these outlandish notions? Do you comprehend exactly what going to bed early means? It means that all the science which has been lavished in the perfection of elec-

tro-lighting has been thrown away; it means
that generous wines and fine tobacco are
not necessary parts of a man's existence; it
means that the art bestowed on the pro-
duction of a good dinner is art misapplied;
it means that jovial sociability amongst
men is a needless requirement; it means
that dice are senseless cubes of ivory; it
means that the game of billiards is on a par
with croquet; it means that the gigantic
intellect which first conceived a pack of
cards laboured only to be scorned and
slighted by the coming generations—in
fact, it means that one gives up every pleasure in life without a murmur. Now, can
such a state of affairs be right? I ask you
candidly and dispassionately—Is there not
something radically wrong in this? Is it
right or just that one must foreswear all
pleasure in order to keep one's health? No,
Grandby—there is no doubt about it—it is
all wrong! The physical condition of the
world does not keep pace with civilisation.
It never progresses—it has never advanced
one step since Eve, in the Garden of Eden,
considered herself fashionably dressed with
merely a string of fig-leaves—and the result

is that life has become unendurable to all
mankind.'

He falls back exhausted, and takes a
strong pull at his peg, and, in consequence
of his recumbent position, he again chokes.

'It is the same in everything,' he continues presently. 'Great or small—it matters not! The solar system is wrong; the
earth's temperature is wrong; the physical
aspect of the world is wrong; men are
wrong; women are wrong; children are
wrong; the whole living creation is wrong,
and the mechanism of the individual's body
is wrong. Great heavens! I become exasperated, as I lie here thinking of this
lamentable state of affairs. My blood literally boils with indignation! To think, for
instance, that one cannot even drink lying
down, without choking! Why is it so?
Why should every portion of one's body
be faulty in construction? Does it not
strike you as extraordinary that in the construction of the human throat such an
evident contingency as that of desiring to
drink in a recumbent position should have
been overlooked? Can any excuse be found
in palliation of such gross carelessness?

No—none—and yet we are expected to receive it in a thankful spirit. Ugh! it's positively disgusting!'

Grandby laughs long and heartily at this outburst. He is intensely amused at the thorough earnestness with which his friend propounds his eccentric ideas. There is no sense of humour underlying his remarks; he means exactly what he says to the very letter, and he lies there, looking and feeling the most miserable and injured of men.

'Well, any how, you have a prospect of excitement to-night,' remarks Grandby, in a cheering tone. 'Your dance will be a change from your daily routine.'

A low groan proceeds from Loftus's mouth, and he hastily sits up, and swallows off his peg.

'Don't mention it—please, don't mention it,' he cries, in tones of pained entreaty. 'What I have suffered with regard to this dance, no man's intellect would be capable of grasping! During the last few days, life has been a perfect burden to me.'

'Ah!—you have been overworked in consequence?'

'Overworked! Words won't express to

you what I have had to undergo. The meetings which we have had have been enough alone to drive an ordinarily constituted individual into his grave. How I have survived them, I cannot understand.'

'I looked into the room as I passed,' remarks Grandby. 'There were a great number of natives there, fighting and jabbering, but they didn't seem to be making progress.'

Loftus gives vent to another loud groan, and then, in a despairing voice, he murmurs,

'I say, old chap, what is the time?'

Grandby looks at the clock on the mantelpiece; the hands point to three o'clock.

'Why—your clock is stopped!'

'Yes—I know; it is always so. I do it on purpose. I hate to see that minute hand crawling slowly round the face—it exasperates and accentuates the dulness of existence. So I set my clock at three—the happiest hour in the day—and I try to imagine that it is always three a.m.; but it requires a very vivid imagination to do so, I can tell you,' he adds, with a dismal shake of the head.

'It is nearly one,' says Grandby, looking

at his watch; 'and, between ourselves, I am feeling uncommonly hungry!'

'Ah! I wish I did,' is the response, 'I have not felt hungry for nine long years, and yet I have been compelled to eat to keep myself alive. I suppose I must get up—the dread moment cannot be postponed further. At the last meeting we held I was deputed to see after the ornamentation of the room, and it is all to be done this afternoon—and I am well-nigh crushed at the thought. Do you see anything outside, old chap?'

Grandby walks to the door and looks out.

'Yes,' he says, 'there are three bile-carts filled with plants, and a crowd of natives—*derzies*, apparently.'

'Oh, Jehoshaphat! was ever man so cursed before!' cries Loftus, sitting up in bed. 'I must get up—I never get a moment's peace—the whole club is topsy-turvy, and even in my private room I can obtain no rest. Don't go, old chap! You must stay and help me—oh, you must! Could anything have been more fortunate than your timely visit?'

This sudden inspiration on the part of Loftus revives him to such an extent that, before he is well aware of the fact himself, he is out of bed, and is standing in front of Grandby, earnestly beseeching him 'not to forsake an old friend in a moment of distress, but to give him a helping hand.'

Grandby willingly assents, with a good-natured smile, thereby transporting Loftus with joy. His delight is so excessive that he gives a very undignified swoop with his right leg in the air, as an expression of his satisfaction; then he opens the door, and pokes out his head, and calls the assembled crowd of natives by the most opprobrious name in the Hindi tongue, which action amuses him so immensely that he laughs aloud at their discomfited faces.

'I shan't be a moment, old chap,' he cries, and he quickly disappears into the bath-room, whence arises a duet of oaths and water-splashing, in which the basso greatly predominates.

In a few minutes he emerges, and begins to rapidly dress in front of the fire, at the same time explaining to Grandby the hardness of his fate.

'The people in this station,' he says, rubbing his hair savagely with a rough towel, 'are unacquainted with the word

content. Such a grumbling, fighting, grasping set I have never met before, and sincerely hope never to meet again. Life is
not long enough to voluntarily undergo such
torture as contact with them evolves, when
they can be avoided. To please them we
determine to give a dance. We go to
every conceivable inconvenience—turn our
house literally upside down, so that we
never have a comfortable meal for a week
together. But they are not contented!
Bless you—no! The floor, which is good
enough for us, is not good enough for
them! It has to be scrubbed, and waxed,
and greased, and polished, made, in fact,
damnably unpleasant and unsafe, just to
please *them*—and one of us unfortunate
devils has to waste his intellect in the preparation of the floor. Then they turn up
their noses at the food! What is good
enough for us, is not good enough for
them. Oh, dear, no! They want mayon-
naise, and chicken aspics, forced-meat beast-
liness and bilious puddings, and, what not
else, God alone knows! And so we have
to form a committee, and degrade our
manhood by calmly sitting down to plan a
supper to suit their fastidious tastes! Not

even the wine meets with their approval! The sherry is too-mild, and the champagne too-dry, so one of us miserable creatures has to demean himself by ordering so many dozen *sweet* champagne. Oh, it is horrible! There is a certain class of woman who frequents these hops, who refuses to drink anything but the very *sweetest* of champagnes, and she drinks such an amount too that I really have a most sincere compassion for her inside on the following morning. And then they must have flowers! Oh, they *must*—they won't come otherwise—paint and paper is revolting to their cultivated gaze. They want flowers and they *will* have flowers, and muslin hangings, and idiotic festoons, and tropical plants, and ferns, and wood-lice! Oh, my heart turns sick when I think of it—their wants are outrageous and inconceivable. Ah! we little knew what we were letting ourselves in for when we were prevailed on to give a dance. But we know now,' he adds, with an impressive shake of the head, 'we know now; yes—we are wiser now—and we will never make such a mistake again, however long we live.'

'I don't doubt that you are very hard-worked,' laughs Grandby. 'At the same time, if such be the case, it seems peculiar that on the day of the dance you are all in bed at noon, for such I conclude to be the case.'

'No wonder that we oversleep ourselves. Our minds and bodies are literally prostrated with their exertions. You have no idea, until you come to do it yourself, what an endless amount of work there is to be done. Who cares what hardships we go through? The people come, and use our floor and band, eat our food and drink our wine, and go away and swear—especially if the next morning they become aware that they must have eaten and drunk too much the night before. My dear Grandby, there is no such thing as gratitude in this world. The sentiment disappeared from the human race when Adam and Eve were kicked out of Eden for indulging in dessert. The punishment was so monstrously unjust and disproportionate to the offence that gratitude was killed for ever. On that remarkable day it died a natural death. You may think that I exaggerate the work we have to do, but I can solemnly assure you that

I don't. Questions of vital importance, which must be settled, crop up day and night. Perhaps you won't believe me, but it is gospel truth—we were up till four o'clock this morning trying to decide whether the raised-pie, which is a *chef-d'œuvre* of culinary art, should be placed at the head or in the centre of the table. You may say that it is a matter of small consequence, but others thought differently —and, as I say, we sat up till four discussing the matter. There were some good speeches made too, by-the-by ; that fellow Bramley was especially caustic on the subject.'

'And on what did you decide finally?' asks Grandby, gravely.

'Well, to tell the truth, we could come to no decision. We were an even number, and half voted for the top of the table, and half for the centre, and no one individual would swerve one atom from his originally expressed opinion. So finally I proposed that it should be left to chance—that no orders should be given about it, and that the butler should place it where he thought best. This was carried unanimously. It was a very lucky thought of mine, for I

fully believe, if I had not made the suggestion, that we should be seated there now.
That fellow Bramley has a wonderful talent
for rhetoric. But come along and have
some lunch, and after we are filled, as you
hope to be saved, lend me a helping hand!'

CHAPTER VII.

A BILLET-DOUX.

WITHIN a few minutes the two young men
are in the breakfast-room, seated at a small,
round table, discussing an appetising little
lunch. To Grandby, whose appetite is
immense after his morning's walk, everything seems to be of the very best, but,
oppressed by the burden of office, Loftus'
spirits are not sufficiently high to allow
him to endorse his friend's opinion. On
the contrary, he makes a point of grumbling at everything. The wines are tart,
the food is beastly, and the butler is a fool!
This latter individual—a wiry little Asiatic,
clothed in European garb—finally is unable
to stand the volleys of abuse which fall
upon his unoffending head, and he beats a
hasty retreat, and positively refuses to
emerge again from his hiding-place.

'He would rather resign his appointment,' he sends word by a native servant.

'Ah! but I will be even with him yet!' growls Loftus, with a vindictive shake of the head.

'Wait till to-morrow, at any rate,' laughs Grandby. 'Don't forget that on that man's opinion depends the position of the raised-pie to-night.'

Loftus grunts. He has half a suspicion that Grandby is chaffing him, and the Dictator of the Doonga Club never allows chaff from anyone, so he immediately changes the subject.

'Mind you be here in time,' he says, 'we shall begin punctually at half-past nine.'

'I am not coming,' says Grandby, quietly; 'I have to be very careful of myself at present, and I cannot run the risk of catching a chill. Besides, I am so weak still that I should never be able to stand it.'

Loftus does not answer him at once. He sits eyeing him steadily with a look of keen curiosity on his face, as though he were studying some strange variety of biped. And then he coughs and sips his madeira thoughtfully, and says, mildly,

'Say that again, please.'

Grandby smiles good-humouredly.

'You seem very surprised,' he says, 'but I am only stating the exact truth. My doctor would have an epileptic fit if he knew that I contemplated going to a dance. Besides, I have really no inclination to come. I am a perfect stranger here, and it would be very dull.'

Loftus continues his scrutiny of Grandby's person for fully half-a-minute, and then he turns away with an expression of incredulous wonder depicted on his face.

'Holy Moses!' he murmurs, *sotto voce*, 'he's a rum 'un, if you like!'

'Why? Is it such a very extraordinary proceeding?' asks Grandby, with amusement; 'I merely wish to retain my health —the loss of which you were only just now lamenting.'

Loftus does not answer. He is apparently lost in speculation. His mind is incapable of grasping Grandby's argument. Such a line of procedure is to him inconceivable—impossible. To willingly renounce the prospect of a night's carouse —for to Loftus the *dance* goes for nothing, as compared to what will follow when the ladies have withdrawn—on the plea of weak health is to him so amazing and incomprehensible that he completely loses his customary volubility of speech.

Grandby is unable to resist laughing at the comical expression of astonishment on his face, and at the sound his friend emerges from his trance. He dashes off his madeira, and hurriedly rises.

'Come to the ball-room,' he says, quietly. 'It is time we were beginning;' and then he shakes his head gravely from side to side, and murmurs to himself, '"Jerusalem the Golden," but he's a rum cove!'

The ball-room presents a very different aspect to what it did an hour ago. In spite of the family feuds which presumably existed amongst the natives engaged in its preparation, they have done their duty like men, and have left it looking very spick-and-span.

A young man dressed in startling *déshabille* is superintending the polishing of the floor, and Loftus greets him with great effusion.

'Well, things are looking up, old chap,' he says, briskly. 'It is only a matter of really putting one's back to it, and the greatest difficulties can be surmounted.

Allow me to introduce you to my friend Grandby. Mr. Grandby—Mr. Bramley.'

Bramley shakes him languidly by the hand, and hopes, in a tone of the supremest indifference, that he is finding himself quite well.

Grandby eyes him curiously. He is a very *blasé*-looking individual, with bleared face and watery eyes, dressed in flannel trousers and flannel shirt, open at the neck, with no tie. In fact, at first sight, he does not impress him as a man possessing any marked talent for rhetoric.

Whether his talents in this respect be imaginary or real, there is not much opening for them in his present occupation, which consists in standing moodily against the wall, watching various natives applying polish to the floor. Occasionally a monosyllabic remark in the vernacular issues from his lips, but it sounds more like an interjection of abuse than a dignified utterance, such as might be expected from a man bearing such a brilliant reputation for elocution.

Presently the natives are ordered to stand up, and Bramley proceeds to inspect their work. He walks up and down the room, bestowing a careful scrutiny on every plank, and then he begins to languidly slide about, to test the slipperiness of the floor. In doing so, his foot suddenly slips away from under him, and, losing his balance, he falls heavily to the ground. But, even in a critical position like this, he shows no special aptitude for fluency of language. His remark is certainly forcible and energetic, but nothing more. He merely says, ' Damn !' in a very loud voice, and then rises from the ground with a perfectly unruffled demeanour.

Grandby turns away to hide his smile. He is not in the least impressed by Bramley's oratorical display, and he is none the more convinced when Loftus draws him aside and whispers to him in a tone of pride, as though he were exhibiting some specimen of rare peculiarity,

' Just look at him ! Have you ever seen his like before ? By Jove, sir, he is a really wonderful creation !'

Under Bramley's direction, the natives now file out, and then ' the wonderful creation ' himself signifies his intention of departing in the longest speech which

Grandby has as yet heard issue from his gifted mouth.

'I am dead-beat,' he says, 'and I must have a peg.' And, without looking round him, he leaves the room.

' You can send one in here for me,' shouts Loftus after his retreating figure. ' And you will have one too, Grandby, won't you?'

There is an air of hesitation about this query. In his eyes, Grandby now has become such a peculiarly-organised individual that he is beginning to feel doubtful how to treat him. His one idea of hospitality was to offer his guests whisky-pegs, and, prior to his meeting Grandby, he had never known the system to fail. The pegs had been accepted, and eagerly drunk, and sociability had been rapidly established. But with Grandby it was all different; he did not even seem to appreciate the spirit of the hospitality. Loftus naturally wished to do the right thing with his guest, for he was grateful beyond expression for Grandby's offer of assistance in the decoration of the room, but how to do it was a question which entirely baffled his sense of understanding. For years he had been swimming in a groove of spirits and aerated water, and he resembled a fish out of water when he found himself suddenly in a different situation.

Grandby declines the proffered drink, and smiles inwardly as he catches the expression of Loftus' face. There is a look of strained anxiety upon it which is really painful to behold. However, Loftus speedily recovers his spirits when he sees the energetic way in which his assistant begins to set about the business in hand. The flowers and plants are brought in from outside, and are then skilfully disposed about the room in various artistic shapes.

Loftus sits, with peg in hand, watching the arrangements with an admiring eye.

'He may be a rum cove,' he mutters to himself; 'but there is not much doubt of him being all there. He is a downright cute 'un.'

Under Grandby's ready guidance, the room rapidly undergoes a transformation; in less than an hour every plant and flower has been placed in position, and the room is ready for use.

Loftus is quite overcome. His solicitude concerning the state of Grandby's health after his exertions is really touching.

'Are you quite sure you feel alright?' he asks. 'Now, hadn't you better just come and sit down. You must be terribly fagged. No wonder that you knock up in the plains, if you work like this. Your energy is stupendous.'

Grandby declines to sit down. He is, in reality, feeling very tired from his recent exertions, and he wishes to get home as soon as possible, so he holds out his hand and says good-bye.

'Are you really going?—Then good-bye, old chap,' cries Loftus, grasping it warmly in return. 'You are a brick—a regular brick! How can I ever thank you? Now, won't you alter your decision, and come this evening?'

'No, thanks,' is the laughing rejoinder; 'with me it is not a matter of choice, but one of necessity.'

'Well, you must come and see me to-morrow, at any rate—any time after one o'clock you will find me up. So good-bye, and—and—you are quite sure'—doubt-fully—'that you won't have a peg?'

'Oh! quite sure,' cries Grandby, laughing heartily; and then he leaves him, and walks as fast as he can in the direction of Banbury's Hotel.

Dinner that night is a very lugubrious repast. There is none of the refined *espièglerie* of the night before. In fact, there is only one lady present—Mrs. Stockton—and she sits on Grandby's right hand, grim and massive.

To his great annoyance, she opens a conversation with him, having first formally introduced herself to him as 'Mrs. Stockton, wife of Colonel Stockton, of the Bengal Cavalry.'

After a few prefatory remarks, she explains to him that the absence of the ladies that night from table was due to their inconceivable vanity, which caused them to require from two to three hours for the purpose of decorating their bodies for the dance. Such deliberate waste of time was literally sinful, for they ought to have known as well as she did that two or three *weeks* of care would have had no effect whatever on their unprepossessing persons. An iron pot did not look like silver because you chose to rub it bright. She herself, she is thankful to say, was above such contemptible weakness. She would rather forego altogether the

doubtful pleasures of the dance, than miss
the solid gratification of a good dinner.
Not that she is vulgarly fond of her food,
she hastens to explain, but merely that on
principle she objects to irregularity in
meals. It is only another way of expressing irregularity in health.

Grandby, not in the least interested in
her remarks, tries his utmost not to show
the same. He is vainly attempting to
form some suitable reply, when she starts
off afresh with the remark that Mrs. Renfrew,—' the scraggy, underbred woman,
you may remember, who sat on the opposite side of the table the night before,'—
had been suddenly taken ill, and was confined to her room in consequence. The
nature of her complaint she did not know,
but it was probably something very low
and vulgar, for she had noticed that she
possessed a very reprehensible habit of
bolting her food. This was the reason of
the woman's absence that night, and
though she was the very last person in the
world to feel vindictively inclined towards
a fellow-Christian, still she could not help
stating—in the strictest confidence, of
course—that she thought Mrs. Renfrew's

absence was preferable to her presence.
She might be wrong in her estimate of that
lady's character—every mortal, of course,
being liable to mistakes—but she could not
help feeling that there was a something
about her which seemed to point to the
fact that she was mean, vulgar, unstable,
and vicious.

Having made these few remarks on Mrs.
Renfrew's person, she states her opinion in
very trenchant language concerning Mrs.
Lamb, begging him to take warning—
from one who bore malice towards no one,
but was actuated solely by motives of Christian charity—and to avoid the lady in
question on every possible occasion; because, as she emphatically states, the
woman is not to be trusted.

With which she launches out into an
exhaustive statement of Mrs. Lamb's fail-
ings, and, having stripped her character to
the very bone, she commences to do likewise to another lady, and then on to a
third, and so on throughout the dinner.

Grandby's disgust is palpably written
on his face, but Mrs. Stockton does not
observe it. On the contrary, she fondly
imagines that she is making a strong im-

pression on the good-looking young man, and she consequently redoubles the force of the stream of invective issuing from her lips.

The dinner breaks up early, and Grandby rises with such a sigh of relief that its import must have been evident to anyone else but Mrs. Stockton.

She, on the contrary, takes it as an expression of regret, and she turns to him, as they are leaving the room, with a smile of gracious affability on her unpleasing countenance.

'We shall meet again to-night, Mr. Grandby,' she says, playfully. 'Mind you come early—there is still a little corner of my card unfilled.'

'I am not going to the dance, Mrs. Stockton,' he says, shortly—almost rudely. 'I will wish you a good-night,' and, without waiting to see the effect of his speech, he turns away and leaves her.

He feels very angry, and he stalks savagely up to his little house. How has that vulgar woman dared to insult all his manliness of spirit and feeling of gentlemanly honour by discussing the characters of other ladies in the low way she has done!

What business is it of his—and what business is it of hers? What does he care concerning the sayings and doings of the other inmates of the hotel, and what does it signify to him whether Mrs. Lamb has taken a bath or not during her three months' sojourn in the Himalayas? He has no wish to be made the confidant of all these scandalous tales! He has come to Banbury's Hotel for rest and quiet, and for no other reason—and, if he cannot obtain it there, he will leave the place immediately.

By the time he reaches his house his temper has quite deserted him, and he kicks open his door with a violent swing of his leg. It is quite dark within, and he gropes about for the matches.

The idea of his going to the dance! He laughs sardonically at the notion. To go out into the cold, and to stay up all night, in order to clasp such a woman as Mrs. Stockton in his arms! What utter bliss! To run the risk of a return of fever in order to hear whether certain ladies wear false hips or patent palpitators! What ecstatic rapture! Go to the dance indeed!

Not if he knows it! Wild horses would not drag him out again to-night!

He finds the matches and lights the lamp, and then with unnecessary vehemence he proceeds to stir up the embers of the fire.

He throws off his coat and walks to the glass for the purpose of unpinning his tie, when suddenly his eye catches sight of an object lying on the dressing-table, which rivets his attention. It is a little billet-doux, tastefully twisted into triangle shape, and by its side is lying a little button-hole —a sweet moss-rosebud, backed with a sprig of maiden-hair fern.

He takes up the note and reads the address.

'Frank Grandby, Esq., Royal Artillery,' written in a clear, angular lady's hand.

He looks at it wonderingly for several moments, vainly striving to imagine what it signifies; and then he hastily tears it open and reads these words:

'Mind you come to the dance—and be punctual.

'D. F.'

CHAPTER VIII.

AT THE DANCE.

' MIND you come to the dance—and be punctual.

'D. F.'

That is all; and yet he continues to stare at the scented scrap of paper, repeating the words over and over again, with a puzzled countenance, as though he were attempting to decipher hieroglyphics of the abstrusest order.

' " Mind you come to the dance—and be punctual, D. F." ' he murmurs vaguely to himself. ' " Mind you come to the dance and be punctual!   Diana Forsdyke." '

What does it mean, he asks himself, in a bewildered way; although the meaning of the little note is clear and evident.   And then he slightly changes the formation of his query, and asks—What does *she* mean?

The moments pass, and still he stands regarding the little note, as though he thought by dint of perseverance he may chance to light on some clue as to the motive of the young lady in sending it to him. That the initials D. F. stand for Diana Forsdyke he has not the smallest doubt! He is not at all exercised on *that* point, but he is puzzled beyond expression as to her reason in writing to *him*—a perfect stranger to her.

It strikes him as a most extraordinary proceeding on the part of a young girl who has outwardly appeared so demure and shy. From her having deliberately committed such a grave breach of etiquette it becomes evident that her reasons for wishing to make his acquaintance must be very strong indeed.

But what can these reasons be? Can it be that she is unhappy, and that she has observed in his looks the feeling of interest which her apparently forlorn lot has awakened in him? Can this be the root of her strange behaviour? Has he been right, after all, in fancying that in her he has discovered a kindred spirit? Is the magnetic fluid in their systems of a similar nature, attracting them towards each other by its own subtle force, irrespective of their minds?

This idea is so extremely pleasant to Frank Grandby that he does not attempt to argue out the matter further. He believes, or rather affects to believe, that he is thoroughly convinced, and he does not hesitate a moment longer. He folds up the note, and places it in his pocket with reverential care, affixes to his coat the little sprig of maiden-hair, finds a pair of gloves, puts on his hat and coat, and sallies forth.

And then he laughs—a merry, rippling laugh. He is so thoroughly honest that he is unable to deceive himself for long; and he knows very well, as he strides down the hill, that his theory concerning the magnetic fluid in Miss Forsdyke's system is merely a soothing-salve to the conscience, and that he is going to the dance not because he is attracted there against his will, but simply in order to make the acquaintance of an extremely lovely girl, who has tickled his vanity by making the first overtures towards him.

That is the true state of the case, and he

laughs to himself at the cunning which he has employed to convince himself that it is his duty to obey the young lady's wish.

'But, all the same,' he thinks, 'there must be something in the matter which does not appear at present. I am not such an ass as to imagine that I have made an impression on her heart. If the law of evolution holds good in *affaires-de-cœur*, girls of the nineteenth century must be more or less case-hardened by this time. So that is nothing to do with it. It must be something else; and my only way of ascertaining the same is to move onward.'

The Mall is ablaze with moving lights, borne in front of the dandies, conveying their fair burdens to the club. Looking down the hill, the scene resembles more some theatrical effect than a high-road on this prosaic earth. The moon has not yet risen, and the darkness above heightens the weird effect of the hundreds of moving figures, with their dark shadows falling grotesquely in the dancing light, all converging on to one point, where the little inclined road leading down to the club leaves the Mall. Here the crush is intense. The night air is broken with the discordant noise of natives yelling at the top of their repellant voices, dandies collide, and women utter timid little shrieks, and all is confusion.

Grandby manages to wedge his way through the mass of struggling human beings, and he soon arrives at the club, breathless with the exertion.

Up till now he has felt as bold as brass. Secretly invited to attend the dance by the fairest lady in the place, he has hastened, with a palpitating heart, to do her bidding; but now, as his foot crosses the threshold of the club, his courage completely deserts him, and he is seized with vague misgivings. Has he been labouring under an hallucination, or is it actual reality that he has received the note?

Without looking to the right or left, preceded by a servant, he hastens to the cloak-room, where he removes his coat and hat. Feverishly his fingers search his waistcoat-pockets, and then a deep sigh of relief escapes him. It is alright! It is no vivid dream of his imagination! It has all actually happened, and the note in question is lying in his hand, and the words, 'Mind you come to the dance—and be punctual! D. F.' are again before his eyes.

He feels so nervous, that no sooner has he dissipated the thought than another enters his mind—one so terrible that he hardly dare breathe it to himself! Supposing—and his heart stands still with very dread—*supposing the whole thing to be a hoax!*

The contemplation of such a possibility is so truly awful, that he turns quite pale. A hoax! Supposing, for instance, that it is a joke on the part of Loftus, or some similar worthy, in order to attract him there, with the purpose of having a good laugh at his expense! He is too agitated to perceive the absurdity, the impossibility, of such a notion. He quite forgets that no one has the faintest conception of the interest he takes in Miss Diana Forsdyke. He has such a rooted horror of being made an object of ridicule, that, on the bare chance of his suspicions being true, he is of half-a-mind to fly back to Banbury's at once. But, before he can fully make up his mind on the point, he becomes conscious of some one entering the room, and, looking into the mirror in front of him, he sees the reflection of the very man at present occupying his thoughts—Vernon Loftus!

In a moment he collects himself. He takes up a hair-brush, and commences to brush his hair with an affectation of easy nonchalance, determined neither to show by word or gesture that the possible hoax has been successful. He watches Loftus' reflection crossing the room, and then their eyes meet, and he sees such a look of un-affected amazement depicted on his friend's face that in a moment all doubt as to his integrity disappears.

'Good Lord!—great God!' is all that Loftus says; and then, as though over-come by the unexpected appearance of his friend, he sinks down into a chair, earnest-ly invoking at intervals his Maker in pet terms of his own.

'Well, I have come after all,' says Grandby, smiling.

'And I am deuced glad to see you,' answers Loftus, with an effort, conquering his astonishment. ' But, by the holy poker, if you aren't the rummest cove in Christen-dom, you may leather me black and blue! What the deuce made you alter your de-cision so suddenly? This afternoon you were so decided on the point that, 'pon my word, old chap, you made me feel quite small.'

Now properly, on being propounded this direct query, Grandby should have hesitated and looked confused. But, to his shame, it must be stated that he does nothing of the sort. Instead, he presents a bold, fearless face, with a smile of ineffable charm upon his lips, and tells a deliberate falsehood with a most convincing airiness of manner.

'Well, to tell the truth, Loftus,' he says, 'I found Banbury's so infernally dull to-night that I felt that I could not do better than follow the example of the rest of the world; so, in the face of my emphatic refusal this morning, I have come. You have me distinctly at a disadvantage, so I trust that you will be lenient towards me.' And then he laughs—one of those soft, gentle laughs, which were found impossible to resist by all who heard them.

Loftus rises and expresses the pleasure which his appearance has given him in the most forcible language of his vocabulary.

'And now, let's go downstairs,' he adds. 'The place is crammed with human flesh.

Let us stand in the doorway, and gloat over the exhibition.'

The two young men leave the room and walk downstairs. From the ball-room issue the strains of the cavalry band quartered for the summer at the Doonga depôt, and the noise of feet sliding over the polished floor breaks upon their ears, showing them that the votaries of the maddening, mazy dance have already begun in earnest. A buzz of female voices, softly modulated, permeates the air, and harmonises with the rustling *frou-frou* of silks and laces, emitting perfumes of the subtlest odours. All Doonga is present, thirsting for enjoyment. Already the room is crowded with languishing couples, revolving in tight embrace to the dulcet sounds, and every moment fresh instalments are arriving, heavily wrapped and cloaked, and disappearing for a moment or so into that mystery of mysteries,—*sanctum sanctorum*,—the lady's cloak-room, and thence re-appearing, fresh and lovely, ready for the fray.

What blushes!—What simperings and playful affectations!—What a world of meaning can be put, by dint of study, into the mere fluttering of a fan! How their fresh young faces brighten and suf-

fuse with carmine as they see the hero of
their dreams approaching them, programme
in hand, to request the pleasure of a dance!
How coquettishly they turn away their
heads, and affect to hesitate, pretending
that their cards are full! And how their
little hearts are palpitating at the success
of their manœuvre! Alas! all this is really
sad to see—so young, and yet so fully
versed in the subtle art of coquetry!

The question which puzzles the masculine mind is from what strange source do
these fair young things derive their perfect
knowledge of the dangerous art? Do their
mothers initiate them into its mysteries
prior to their launch into the vortex of
the seething world of fashion? Or is
it the duty of the governess to instruct
their pupils in the art? Or is it inherent
to them—born in them—inseparable from
their flesh and blood? Who knows, except
those behind the scenes? What man can
say, without fear of refutation, that Eve
threw herself bodily at first sight into
Adam's arms, without first attempting to
enhance her charms by a tantalising affectation of coyness and maiden modesty?

Loftus, in the doorway, is gloating to
his heart's content. Nothing can escape

his wary eye, and a running commentary
on his surroundings issues from his mouth.

'Oh, great Cæsar!' he cries, 'there is
Mrs. Lamb dancing with her husband!
Can't get anyone else, I suppose—and no
wonder! Poor devil, how I pity him!
Look at them, Grandby. Did you ever
see anything to equal the expression on
her face? Dying duck in a thunderstorm,
eh? If she doesn't suggest to you a box
of liver-pills, you may leather me black
and blue!'

Grandby makes no answer beyond a
feeble smile. In fact, he is totally unconscious of what his companion is saying.
His mind is running on his little *billet-doux*,
and his eyes are seeking in and out among
the dancers for the young lady whose sig-
nature it bears. But he is unsuccessful in
his search; amidst that throng of laughing
girlhood he can discern no Miss Diana
Forsdyke.

'Why, if there isn't old Mother Stockton!' cries Loftus, in huge delight at the
discovery. 'Her fringe is fuller and more
fascinating than ever, I declare! Have
you ever seen such a woman in your life?
Fourteen stone, if she's a pound; forty

round the girth, and distinctly aged, and yet expecting to be trotted out! Look at her smiling and smirking over there. She will wag her fringe off in a minute, if she isn't careful. Who the deuce is she nodding to in that violent fashion? Oh, my hat! it's that chap Bramley, and—and he is actually asking her to dance! Well, if he hasn't the pluck of a blue-devil, you may blow me to smithereens!'

But Grandby does not hear a word. His whole attention is riveted on the further corner of the room, where he has discovered the object of his search, sitting alone, unnoticed by the crowd. She is dressed in a white *tulle* costume of the waterfall order, with a knot or two of neutral tint about her skirts and bodice, and her red-gold hair is brushed up and is neatly arranged on the top of her head after the old Greek style. There is an air of melancholy on her lovely face strangely out of keeping with the gladsome scene, and her hands are lying listlessly on her lap, and her eyes are drooped, so that she sees none of the dancing throng whirling round and round the room. She looks lonely, wretched, miserable, and Grandby's warm young heart fills with a great compassion, and he impulsively makes a step towards her.

'Don't go, old chap,' says the voice of Loftus; 'you haven't answered my question yet.'

'I—I beg your pardon,' he stammers, 'I did not quite hear what you said.'

'I was saying—supposing, now, you were on a desert island with Mother Stockton and Mrs. Lamb as your sole companions—and you suddenly felt a yearning after the married state. Which of the two would you take to your manly bosom?'

'Oh, good gracious!' laughs Grandby, 'God forfend that I should ever be placed in such a predicament!'

'Yes, you are right—it would be an awkward position to find oneself in,' says Loftus, gravely considering the case. 'To a sensitive temperament like my own, either of those females would mean certain death. It would therefore resolve itself into a question of bachelorhood or death, and I think that I should have no hesitation in choosing the former. Heavens alive! if there ain't Miss Forsdyke!' and, before Grandby can make reply, he has left his side, and is moving off in the direction of the girl.

Loftus bravely fights his way towards her, regardless of the scowls cast on his intrepid figure by the irate dancers whom his rapid progress has inconvenienced.

Grandby fixes his eye upon Miss Forsdyke, and he sees her suddenly jump up without a shade of colour in her face. Loftus is before her with outstretched hand, but she does not seem to see it. To Grandby, who is following intently her every movement, she appears to have received a sudden shock. A wave of agitation sweeps across her dead-pale face, and she makes a gesture as though to ward off a coming blow.

Loftus bends forward and whispers in her ear, and gradually the half-scared expression leaves her face, and she slowly extends her hand, with a forced smile upon her lips. What does it mean? Have his eyes deceived him, or is it the fact that what he has imagined to have seen has actually happened?

The whole thing has been so momentary that, before he can decide whether his imagination has played him false or not, he sees the couple standing up, apparently on the very best of terms, and then they leave the side of the room and join the dancers.

'What a fool I am!' he mutters. 'My illness has so unstrung my nerves that I positively cannot trust my own senses now. If I continue much longer in this chronic state of hallucination, I shall begin to think that I am either hysterical or working up for delirium tremens.'

The valse comes to an end, and the couples wander out to partake of flirtation, mild and otherwise, in the corridors and balconies. The centre of the room becomes deserted, and all around the sides appear the ghastly array of wall-flowers, sighing, like Mariana of world-fame, for the man who does not choose to come; and they each affect to be engaged in most animated conversation, thereby intimating to outsiders that it is solely a matter of choice that they sit out, instead of dance. And how well, too, they do their parts! How they laugh, and attract attention to their persons! With what a charming coyness of glance their eyes wander round

the room in search of a likely victim!
How sprightly is their tongue! How arch
and playful their childlike little ways!

Grandby continues to stand moodily in
the doorway. The thought again strikes
him that this *billet-doux* is nothing but a
hoax. The idea of the young lady having
written to him becomes more and more
improbable each moment that he considers
the case. He feels that he has been fooled
—that he has walked into the snare laid
for him with a lamb-like simplicity—and
the thought does not tend to raise his
spirits. The idea that probably some one
unknown to him is standing near him
watching him and laughing at the success
of his practical joke irritates him intensely.
He is of half-a-mind to go; but, before he
has fully made up his mind on the point,
his pride steps in and asserts itself, and
he determines to brave it out to the last,
and to show by not so much as a gesture
that he has been taken in.

So he casts off the feeling of melancholy
which oppresses him, and takes a steady
stare round the room. The first person
who catches his eye is Mrs. Stockton, and

she immediately waves her fan, beckoning him to approach her. With a groan of disgust, he advances towards her.

'Oh, you naughty young man!' she cries, playfully tapping him with her fan, 'how could you say that you were not coming?'

But Grandby is not in a vein to appreciate elephantine humour, so he does not reply to her in a corresponding tone.

'I only told you what was the truth,' he says. 'At the time I spoke it was my fixed determination *not* to come.'

'And yet you have come! Oh, Mr. Grandby, *do* tell me who it is.'

'Who it is? To what are you referring?'

His tone is certainly not conciliatory, but she does not seem to notice it. She continues, with persuasive archness,

'Now, come—confess! Isn't there a young lady in the question? You can't deceive me, you wicked young man.'

Immediately he is on his guard. Possibly it may be this vindictive old woman who has perpetrated the hoax.

'I can assure you that you are quite mistaken,' he says, lightly, conquering his desire to tell her forcibly to mind her own business. 'It was a sudden impulse which brought me here—and now a sudden impulse is going to take me home again.'

She opens her programme and scans its contents.

'Dear me!' she says, in a tone of surprise, 'if the next dance isn't a square dance! The lancers too! Don't you ever dance the lancers, Mr. Grandby? Now, no denial—I am sure you do!'

'Never—never—never!' he cries, hurriedly breaking in, and throwing politeness to the winds, and with a bow he turns away and leaves her with all possible haste.

What an escape! He takes out his handkerchief, and wipes his brow, inwardly thanking his stars that he has possessed sufficient strength of mind to extricate himself from such a horrible predicament.

The band strikes up again and the room rapidly refills. The wall-flowers become more animated than ever as the sombre black coats file in and look around them for suitable companions. The dancing whirl begins afresh with unflagging energy, but the one figure which Grandby is searching for does not appear. She and her partner have not obeyed the summons of the music.

Mrs. Lamb is standing at the head of a lancers-square beside her husband, and this gallant officer is wearing on his face an expression of hopeless misery which is laughable to behold. Mechanically he moves through the figure, blundering at every step, whilst his bilious spouse, with head erect and mincing gait, shows off all her charms to a non-admiring crowd.

Mrs. Stockton is not dancing. She is sitting, grim and defiant, against the wall, and, as Grandby catches her eye, she scowls across at him with an expression of the deadliest venom on her face, at which, however, he is not in the least concerned. For he is now in a state of mind utterly callous to such a triviality as that of having offended a rude old woman. Feeling very low-spirited, he leans against the door, inwardly cursing everything and everybody, and especially his own folly in having come on such a wild-goose chase.

He wonders what pleasure the dancers find in walking through their steps! He wonders how their faces would look, divested of their thick layer of society varnish! He wonders whether they know what idiots they all look as they stand there bowing and bobbing to each other indiscriminately.

In fact, he is beginning to feel very cynical and ill-tempered. A sense of his having been badly used overcomes him, and a gesture of irritation escapes him.

'Keep your hair on, old chap!' says a mocking voice behind him. 'Never lose your temper!' and looking round he finds Loftus by his side.

'Why aren't you dancing, eh?' asks Loftus. 'What are you doing, standing here, looking as grumpy as a *gruyère* cheese? Come, rouse yourself, and put on that languishing, fascinating leer which is so telling with the ladies. There is a young lady here on whom you have made a great impression, and she wishes to be introduced to you. Yes, my boy, you have made a conquest, though, 'pon my word, it is hardly fair of me to tell you so point-blank. But I always was a darned bad hand at the diplomatic line.'

'I shall be delighted,' says Grandby, indifferently, with the air of a grand duke. 'May I ask the young lady's name?'

'Miss Forsdyke; she is a pretty little thing in white and—and some other sort of colour.'

It has come at last! For the life of him he is unable to prevent the flush of warm colour which lights up his olive-skin.

'I am at your service,' he says, and immediately Loftus starts off, and wends his way towards the ante-room. Grandby follows, with his heart in his mouth. And then he sees her, sitting by herself, pale and subdued, with her eyes directed on the floor.

Loftus advances towards her, and introduces his friend.

'Miss Forsdyke—Mr. Grandby,' he says, with an elaborate bow.

There is not a trace of recognition on her face as she rises and makes him a distant bow. He opens his programme, and makes the conventional idiotic mumble, which is to be construed into a request to have the pleasure of a dance.

'With pleasure,' she says, softly. 'Will the next one suit? It is a valse. The band has stopped, so we can be moving.'

He offers her his arm, and together they move into the ball-room.

CHAPTER IX.

MISS DIANA FORSDYKE.

THE music has not begun as they enter the room, so they stand together by the wall, waiting for the coming strains.

There is an awkward silence. Miss Forsdyke, toying listlessly with her fan, makes no advances, and Grandby feels so painfully confused that he is unable to volunteer a syllable. The silence presently becomes so oppressive that he blurts out the first idea which enters his head. It is by no means a brilliant remark, but it serves its purpose in breaking the ice.

'Isn't the floor nice!' he says, with an affectation of rapture, though, as a matter of fact, he has not tried it.

'Yes, capital,' she says, softly, without looking him in the face.

There is every prospect of another awful

pause, so Grandby, with an effort, attempts to pursue the interesting topic of conversation.

'It is so nice to find a polished floor in India, isn't it ?' he says.

'Yes, very nice,' she answers, placidly, studying the workmanship of her fan.

This is really too dreadful ! If the band does not begin soon, he will have to turn tail and run.

'You don't often meet with one out here, do you ?' he continues, desperately.

'No, not often,' she replies, with exasperating indifference.

Oh! this is positively unendurable! What in the name of all that is holy delays the band ?

'They are a long time striking up,' he says.

'I am sorry that you find it long,' she answers.

'I—I—beg your pardon,' he stammers, confusedly. 'I didn't mean anything rude, I can assure you.'

'Please don't mention it. I am quite certain that it was unintentional.'

A long pause.

'Have you been long in Doonga?' he asks, faintly.

'Just a week to-day. I am staying at Banbury's Hotel.'

That is rather an unnecessary piece of information, he thinks, as he looks blankly in her face. But her next remark literally staggers him.

'Are you living at the club?' she asks.

What a question! Can he be dreaming? For some moments he is literally unable to answer her simple question. Then he manages to mumble, inarticulately,

'No—no—not at the club. I am at Banbury's.'

'Really!' she says, in a tone of surprise. 'I suppose that you have only just come, as I do not remember to have seen you there.'

Not seen him, when he feels half convinced that the note in his pocket has been penned by her fair hand. Either he or she must be downright mad!

'Your memory must be very faulty,' he begins, with a touch of resentment in his tones.

'Yes, it is,' she answers, quickly, 'and so are your manners.'

A burning blush suffuses his whole countenance. He is completely dumbfounded by her manner. It is plainly evident that the covert smiles and significant looks which he has fancied she has cast towards him have existed only in his own imagination. He feels very small and shame-faced, as he stands there, recalling into what terrible errors his overweening vanity has led him, and he thanks his stars that he has not already referred to the little *billet-doux*. He has now no glimmer of doubt that it has been a hoax. His reverie is broken by Miss Forsdyke speaking.

'Are we going to dance, Mr. Grandby?' she says, in an irritated voice. 'The band has been playing for the last two minutes, and if you do not intend to waltz—I should like to sit down.'

With a hurried apology, he passes his arm around her waist, and in the next minute they are whirling round and round to the dulcet strains.

In a moment everything is forgotten. Miss Forsdyke dances divinely, and, as he sweeps round the room, clasping her in his arms, all traces of irritation vanish from his mind. Their steps agree to perfection, and he gives himself up wholly to the

intoxicating influence of the dance. It is
beautiful! It is heavenly! It is divine!

He feels no wish for conversation. As
they glide lightly along to the ever-vary-
ing music, now rising to strains of jubi-
lant grandeur, now sinking into melody of
heartbreaking pathos, a sense of great contentment steals across him. For the moment, he becomes totally oblivious to the
presence of others in the room. His fair
partner is all in all to him, and he bends
down and drinks in the subtle fragrance
of her hair. She is very beautiful! With
half-closed eyes, he scans her faultless profile, and notices the brilliant whiteness of
her skin, and involuntarily his arm tightens
round her waist, as he skilfully steers her
through the labyrinth of dancers.

She, too, has given herself up wholly to
the enjoyment of the moment. He notes
the sparkle in her eye, and the flush upon
her cheek, testifying to the fact; and his
heart grows very tender, and he bends
down over her and whispers in her
ear,

'Is not this perfect happiness?'

She looks up at him with a smile of
ineffable softness on her lips, but she says

nothing, and, as their eyes meet, a sudden thrill seems to pierce his heart.

On and on they go! The music changes from key to key, the melodies rise and fall in strains of melting tenderness, and still they do not stop! In the excitement of the moment, his bodily weakness has deserted him, and he feels strong enough to pursue for ever his present occupation.

But all things—pleasure or pain—must have an end, and presently the last chords of that matchless valse are heard, and the dance is finished. And, as the magic sounds of the music die away, the charm is broken, and the knowledge of his true position returns to him, and he remembers that his partner is no inseparable part of his existence, but a young and lovely girl to whom he is a perfect stranger. Oh! thou great and wondrous strain of Harmony. Thou standest alone, for thou of all known influences art capable of changing joy to sadness, and sorrow into joy!

She looks up to him with a smile of gratitude on her face.

'Thank you, so much,' she whispers, softly. 'Never in my life have I enjoyed a dance so much before.'

'I am afraid that I have tired you very much,' he says.

'Oh! not at all,' she answers, quickly. 'I would not have stopped for worlds. Give me your arm, and take me outside— the room is very warm.'

They leave the room together, and stroll out into the verandah. The moon has risen, and is shedding its silvery tint over the surrounding hills, and the grandeur of the scene before them is silent and impressive. Dark, black shadows of gigantic length, cast by the huge, projecting boulder rocks, fall across the pale-blue stretches of soft moonlight, and the sombre gloom of the great ravine is illumined by the scintillating waters of the mountain stream.

They both stand gazing down into the depths in silence, Grandby's heart feeling soft and tender under the irresistible influence of the beautiful scene, robed in the soft hues of night. Half-way down the opposite hill is a dense cloud-bank, closely hugging the side—lying there in mid-air, calm and white, emblem of peace and purity—and Grandby's eyes are riveted on the same, with his thoughts far away from his surroundings. Through some strange labyrinth of correlative ideas, his thoughts have wandered to the contemplation of the possibility of an after-life.

In these days of advanced free-thought, it is almost impossible for any man to arrive at the age of understanding, without having heard at some time or other in his young life doubts cast on the truth and reality of everything that was held dear and sacred by his buried forefathers. His Bible is despised; his religion ridiculed, and his God is denied.

And Grandby had been no exception to the rule. There had come a time when he had had to pass through the fiery furnace of doubt and mistrust—when all the beliefs of his childhood had been assailed by cold, dispassionate logic, which tore aside the glamour of his ancient faith, and exposed its weak points naked to the eye. But he had emerged from the ordeal, if not scathless, radically unharmed. He was no logician—he thoroughly appreciated how vastly inferior, mentally, he was to those great philosophers who prove point by point that everything is nothing—his mind was utterly incapable of refuting their weighty reasoning. But yet their course of argument did not convince him. His innate sense of reverence, and his sound common-sense refused to accept their theories regarding life and man, and he wrestled long and earnestly with the demon tempter, and triumphed in the end. But it had been only a half-won victory. It had been gained more by dint of avoiding the enemy, than by boldly challenging it to fight. Though the subject was deadly attractive to him, from that moment he studiously avoided it, for he feared its in-fluence on his mind. But on occasions, when strangely moved, he often found him-self half-unconsciously pondering on the subject.

And so it is on this particular evening, as he gazes forth on the majesty of night that a sudden conviction seizes him, and he murmurs to himself, 'How can I doubt such a speaking truth?'

For the moment he has forgotten his companion—forgotten even the memory of that ecstatic dance. She recalls herself to him by addressing him in her gentle voice.

'What do you doubt?' she says, looking up into his face. 'To what are you referring?'

He recovers himself with a start.

'I beg your pardon, Miss Forsdyke,' he answers, hurriedly. 'I am afraid that I have been very rude. It is an awkward habit of mine to fall into a reverie, oblivious to everything around me.'

'Who can wonder at it,' she whispers, 'on such a night as this—with such a glorious scene before us. Will you tell me the subject of your thoughts?'

'I am afraid that they would have no interest for you,' he returns, with a little laugh.

'Ah! but you are mistaken,' she says, softly—and he fancies that her hand tightens on his arm. 'In some unaccountable way, anything you say or do has a strange interest for me. Perhaps you think it peculiar of me to make such a statement, but my nature is very blunt, and I cannot help myself from speaking out my thoughts.'

She heaves a little sigh, and then continues, with a pretty, pleading gesture,

'Tell me, Mr. Grandby, of your thoughts. You seem doubtful on some subject. Confide in me, and we will put our heads together and attempt to arrive at some satisfactory conclusion;' and she laughs a little sadly.

What young man of warm blood and ardent fancy can resist the pleading of a lovely girl, praying for his confidence? As she speaks Grandby feels his pulses quicken, and he hesitates no longer to do her bidding. It is a trivial request to accede to, certainly, but great events often arise from trivial commencements, and great catastrophes sometimes happen, born of the most trifling circumstances. And, in doing her bidding so readily, Grandby, by showing the weakness of his mind, unconsciously wove the first loop of the snare, which afterwards enveloped him almost to destruction.

'Since you command, I obey,' he says, gallantly. 'But at the same time I must warn you that you will be grievously disappointed. My thoughts were running on a subject in no way connected with dancing, dress, or social gaiety.'

'I am sorry that you judge me by such a low standard,' she answers, quietly, with that same touch of sadness in her voice that he has already noticed. 'I hope that you give me credit for being capable of

M 2

taking interest in higher things than dress or social gaiety. Life is not wholly a path of roses. The brambles and thorns are sufficiently prominent to make one at times forget the fragrance of the flowers.'

He looks down at her quickly. Her tone is so different from that of most young girls of her age that his interest in her personality appreciably increases. There is such a genuine ring of pathetic sadness in her voice that he feels assured he has been right in his conviction that her life is far from being happy.

'Your words surprise me, Miss Forsdyke,' he says. 'Surely you, on the very brink of life, have not yet encountered its thorns and brambles?'

'I am twenty-one,' she answers, quietly and decisively, as though the mention of the fact were sufficient to convince him of the contrary. 'Twenty-one years!' she continues, in a dreamy tone, looking upwards at the wide expanse of heaven, 'twenty-one long years of care and toil and trouble. Ah! Mr. Grandby,' she cries, turning impulsively towards him, 'how can you think so strangely on the subject? Do you really mean that this is only the beginning of real life ? If that be so, I dare not contemplate the end.'

There is a silence of several moments. Miss Forsdyke, with her head averted from his gaze, is looking down on the silvery stream, and he, for his part, is too embarrassed to frame a syllable.

They are alone on the balcony. The joyous music is pealing forth again within, and all have gone to its imperious call.

He feels that it devolves on him to answer her with some appropriate words, but his mind and tongue refuse to frame anything suitable to the occasion. What can he say to her ? How can he offer to console her knowing nothing of her life ?

He looks down at her half-averted face, and he notices that her lips are quivering with suppressed emotion. He tries to fathom the reason for her sadness ; he tries to collect his thoughts and imagine to himself some coherent explanation of her strange melancholy ; but he fails. He is incapable of grasping the situation ; he can assign no reason for that peculiar ring of sadness which permeates her tone. That, in spite of her youth and sex, she has suffered greatly he feels convinced, and impulsively he determines to offer himself as her friend, in the hope that he may, by his ready sympathy, alleviate her sorrow.

But, before he has time to speak, she turns and addresses him.

'Pray forgive me, Mr. Grandby,' she says, laying her hand upon his arm, with a half-smile upon her lips. 'It is very selfish of me to speak like this. I am afraid that I am a little depressed to-night. It is a peculiarity about my nature to be invariably seized with melancholy whenever I am expected to be especially gay. I hope that I have not been detaining you. In the contemplation of the star-lit heavens I had quite forgotten social etiquette. It does not do to indulge in reverie,' she adds, with a charming grace; 'it makes one absent-minded. Had we not better return to the ball-room? Probably some young lady is beginning to feel rather bitter at your absence.'

'That is not the case, I can assure you,' he says, with a little laugh. 'I am a perfect stranger here. In fact, my programme is literally blank. If you have no objection, I should prefer occupying those two seats I see at the end of the verandah. There

is nothing so depressing as to find oneself
a perfect stranger in the midst of a joyous
throng.'

'You find that, do you?' she asks,
quickly. ' *You* experience that feeling of
utter melancholy? Ah! I am so glad to
meet with a kindred spirit. Yes, let us go
and sit down where you suggest. I feel
no inclination to dance again.'

He offers her his arm, and they slowly
move towards the far end of the verandah,
which makes a right-angled turn round
the corner of the house, thereby concealing the two low arm-chairs from observation from the front. They seat themselves
side by side.

CHAPTER X.

A MOONLIGHT NARRATION.

GRANDBY is the first to break the silence. He feels quite at his ease with his fair companion in this secluded spot, and he leans towards her and says, in a joking tone,

'You were very hard on me, Miss Forsdyke, when I was first introduced. I was really afraid to open my mouth.'

A soft ripple of laughter issues from her lips. 'I am so sorry,' she says, placing the tips of her fingers on his arm; ' but I really could not help myself. I was so thoroughly ashamed of myself for the moment that, to cover my embarrassment, I took refuge in rudeness. I trust that you will forgive me.'

'There is nothing to forgive,' he says. 'I admit that my remarks were commonplace enough to irritate a saint; but it is no easy art to be able to burst forth into familiar conversation on first introduction to a stranger. But what reason had you to be ashamed? Have you committed some dreadful crime?'

Instead of answer to the point, she makes a very irrelevant reply. A witching smile illumines her *mignonne* face, and she bends forward, and appears to scrutinize his coat.

'What a very charming button-hole you have, Mr. Grandby,' she remarks. 'Where did you manage to get such an exquisite rosebud?'

A slight flush lights up his face, and he commences to stammer out some vague reply.

'Now, sir, no fibs,' she cries, holding up her forefinger in pretty playfulness. 'It is no good your attempting to deceive me, for I happen to know exactly where you got it from—so you had better confess at once, and tell me the clean truth. Come, sir, no prevarication!'

All trace of sadness has disappeared from her face. She is once more the little fairy who welcomed him to Banbury's Hotel on his arrival.

'Since you know the truth,' he says, still blushing, 'it would be needless for me to tell it you. Let me turn the tables, and ask *you* for an explanation.'

'Oh! certainly,' she answers, lightly, 'if you wish it, I will relate the circumstance to you in every detail. But I must warn you that it is a tale of immodesty and shocking impropriety, and you do well to blush even before it is begun.'

'I am not blushing,' he says, blushing furiously.

'Oh! really!' she laughs. 'Thank you for the information; it was a very stupid mistake of mine. The climate of Doonga, then, has done wonders in the improving of your complexion in the last two days. When I first saw you against that tree, you were not so highly coloured. But to my tale! Now listen, and check me if I go wrong.'

She settles herself comfortably down into the low arm-chair, and, holding up one finger, she begins to speak.

'Once upon a time,' she says, 'there was a young man as beautiful as the sun——'

'I object—I object,' interposes Grandby. 'You are wrong to begin with.'

'As beautiful as the sun,' repeats Miss Forsdyke, imperturbably; 'and kindly don't make frivolous objections, Mr. Grandby. Well, this young man once started on a long journey. In course of time he arrived at a beautiful city, built on the slopes of a lovely hill, and there he determined to rest his wearied limbs, for he had travelled far that day. So he made his way to the principal rest-house in the city, and there demanded house-room for the night, which was immediately granted to him. Am I right so far, Mr. Grandby?' she asks, suddenly.

'Quite right,' he answers, laughing heartily. 'I envy you your powers of narration. Pray proceed.'

'Well, up till now,' she says, 'the story has not been hard to tell. There has not been a single word in it to bring the blush to a maiden's countenance; it has breathed nothing but peace and virtue. But unfortunately there is a very dark page to be narrated, and it requires time and judgment on the part of the narrator to give it a presentable appearance.'

She pauses, and places her finger thoughtfully on her lips. The moon is shining down full upon her face and neck, giving a dazzling brilliancy to the fairness of her skin, and his eyes are fixed upon her winsome form with a look of unconcealed admiration on his face. A sense of indescribable contentment steals across him as he fully realises the charm of his present situation—alone in the moonlight, listening to the playful banter of a lovely girl.

After a few moments' consideration, she resumes her narrative.

'Now it happened,' she says, quietly, 'that in this very same rest-house there dwelt a maiden who was so unfortunate as to have been born plain.'

'I object—I strongly object,' he cries, with energy.

'To have been born plain,' repeats Miss Forsdyke, stoutly.

'I really can't allow that,' says Grandby, laughing.

'But you must; there is no question about it. It is the story—and you can't alter the story to suit your own tastes.'

'Pardon me,' he says; 'it is my duty to check you if you go wrong. You have made such a grave mistake that I cannot consent to overlook it.'

'Well, as the story must be told, we can waste no time in wrangling. Under protest, I consent to erase the sentence.'

' And I will supply one in its place. The story should run as follows—" In this very same rest-house there dwelt a maiden, pure and lovely as the Queen of Night." '

A low laugh issues from Miss Forsdyke's lips.

' You are taking a most unwarrantable liberty with the original score, Mr. Grandby,' she says, 'but, to prevent further argument, I will admit it. She was as pure and lovely as the Queen of Night.'

' Ah ! that's much better.'

' You need not make unnecessary interruptions, let me remind you,' she says, with a mischievous twinkle in her eye. ' Now, kindly give me your close attention. It happened that this young maiden had the great misfortune to be far from happy. Her mother was dead, and, through force of circumstances, she was separated from her father, and was living with his sister and her husband. Now, these two relatives were, possibly unintentionally on their parts, harsh and unkind to her. There was nothing kindred between her and them,

and her sensitive nature recoiled from the
uncongeniality of her surroundings. Her
lot was very hard. It seemed to be her
fate that everything she said or did should
be misinterpreted and misunderstood. She
was possessed of a nature capable of loving
deeply, and yet her every overture towards affection was repulsed. She was
denied all the pleasures of youth ; she was
given to understand at every moment that
she was disliked ; she was not trusted; a
system of surveillance was instituted over
her every action, and she was compelled to
give account of every moment of the day.
Am I not right so far ?'

'I cannot say,' says Grandby, gravely;
'I sincerely hope not.'

'Unfortunately one cannot alter a written story according to one's hopes and
fancies,' says Miss Forsdyke, smiling sadly.
'I am relating the story as I read it, without addition or omission. But to continue. Life at last became so irksome to
this young maiden that she felt that she
could endure it no longer. Anything
would be better, she thought, than that
life of dull antagonism, so she determined
to run away. But this she found to be

impossible. She had no money—she had no friends—she was helpless, crushed, alone in the great harsh world.'

A trace of agitation breaks the dull monotony of her tones. He fancies in the moonlight that he can discern a tear standing on her eyelashes, and he turns away his head, for he is feeling strangely moved by her recital. But in a moment she has recovered herself, and she again continues in the same dispassionate tones.

'Well, about this time,' she says, 'the young man as beautiful as the sun appeared. They met at the evening meal, and the young maiden fancied that she could discern a look of pity in the young man's glance. Whether she was right or not, I cannot say, for——'

'She was quite right,' interposes Grandby, quickly; 'I can vouch for that. Pray proceed—you interest me deeply.'

'Well, fancying this, she conceived a sudden interest in the youth, for she was deeply touched at his compassion. She felt that his heart must be indeed good and great if he could thus readily sympathise with a perfect stranger; so she resolved—and now comes the shocking part of my narration—she resolved, on the impulse of the moment, to court his friendship. It was improper—it was immodest —but she did it all the same; for her unhappiness was past endurance, and she yearned for the establishment of a perfect friendship with some other human being. I need not ask you, Mr. Grandby, your opinion of the maiden's conduct—you condemn her utterly?'

'You are mistaken, Miss Forsdyke,' he answers, quietly. 'She did right, and I admire her for her action.'

'It is very soothing to hear you say so,' she answers, softly, 'for I was sadly afraid that, when I arrived at this portion of my story, my heroine would find disfavour in your eyes. But, since you tell me to the contrary, I will continue with restored assurance. It happened that a great *fête* was to be held one night, and the maiden, thinking that probably the young man would attend, expressed a wish to go. This, of course, was denied to her. She used all her persuasive powers to induce her aunt to accede to her request—she even resorted to cunning in feigning a passionate tenderness towards her relative

—but without success; she was rudely refused, and told to stay at home. The maiden was in despair, but the gods had not completely forsaken her, for help suddenly came to her from an unexpected quarter. It chanced that one of the nauseous peculiarities of her guardian's husband was a passion for high living, and he, hearing that a banquet of surpassing excellence had been prepared to grace the *fête*, determined to attend. Now he feared his wife, for her tongue was very sharp and bitter, and he dared not expose himself to her contempt by confessing to the true motive of his wish to go; so he dissembled, and, taking upon himself a parent's love, vehemently maintained that it would be a cruel deed not to allow the maid to go, and, after much resistance from his spouse, he ultimately prevailed; and then the maid was very glad, for she saw a prospect of meeting the young man. Do you follow me?'

'Yes, perfectly. I am more than interested.'

'Well, listen to the conclusion. Accidentally the maiden heard that the young man had expressed his intention not to

go, and then a great grief assailed her, for
all her hopes were shattered to the ground,
and, without thinking what she did, she
sat herself down and wrote to him a note,
begging him to come. *Now* do you not
condemn her?'

'She was quite right,' says Grandby,
firmly. 'Her conduct merits approval,
not condemnation. Is that all?'

'Nearly all. You see, she argued thusly,
saying to herself, "Alone am I in the
world, homeless, friendless, helpless. If I
be right in my suspicion of a great affinity
existing between us two, then he will
come, and I shall gain a friend. If I be
wrong, he will give my note the contempt
which it deserves, and will pay no heed to
its request, and I shall be no worse than
before; for the contempt of one individual
is of little consequence when the whole
world despises one." Possibly you may
think that she argued thus subtly in order
to ease her conscience in the despatching
of the note. But there you do her wrong.
She was unable to resist the impulse within
her which prompted her to write, and,
though fully alive to the gravity of the

step, she accomplished it, and sent it, because she could not help herself.

'At this point, Mr. Grandby,' she says, with a sad smile, 'the manuscript ends, so I unfortunately cannot tell you whether she was right or wrong in her suspicion.'

He leans forward and takes her hand, and imprints on it a reverential kiss. He is visibly agitated as he speaks.

'Can you have any doubt?' he asks, earnestly. 'Does not intuition tell you the conclusion of the story? Do you not know, in your heart, that she was right?'

She withdraws her hand from his grasp, leans forward, and covers her face.

'The story has always touched me very deeply,' she whispers. 'Perhaps there is something similar between my own life and that of the young maiden. I have always hoped and hoped that she was right.'

'And now you know it for a certainty, Miss Forsdyke'—and he is speaking very gravely now—'let us drop the parable, and look the matter boldly in the face. You have honoured me to-night with your confidence, and it is only fair that I should now confide in you. You were right in suspecting me of taking an interest in your being—from the very first moment that I saw you I became confident that there existed between us a subtle bond of sympathy; and it was so strong on my part that I felt myself impelled involuntarily towards you. Intuitively I understood that you were not happy, and I resolved in my heart, provided I obtained the opportunity, to do my utmost to help to brighten your life. How I should have effected the matter I cannot say, but luckily what then seemed impracticable has now been made realisable by your kindness this evening in meeting me half-way. Miss Forsdyke, let us be friends! We are both lonely individuals. Your life is hard, and mine is sombre enough, God knows. Let us combine, and form a great, platonic friendship, and smooth away the difficulties of life with mutual sympathy and advice. I trust that you do not think me presumptuous in speaking to you like this.'

He tries to take her hand. With a passionate gesture she turns from him, and covers her face with her hands, and in another moment he hears her softly weeping.

'Miss Forsdyke, Miss Forsdyke!' he pleads, in an agitated voice, 'I implore you to compose yourself. If I have offended you——'

'Offended!'—she looks at him full in the face with her large, tearful eyes—'offended! Oh! Mr. Grandby, how can you imagine such a thing? How can I thank you for your brave, noble words? I am so unused to kindness that you touch me to the quick. I thought that you would despise me for what I have done?'

'Let us understand one another once for all,' he answers, gravely. 'There is no question of contempt on either side—we have both experienced a desire for a mutual friendship with one another, and we have both met each other half-way. There is much that is similar in our characters; there is much that is similar in our lives. Why should we ignore this elective force which is attracting us together? Why should we not take advantage of it by the formation of a great friendship on pure platonic lines, from which we may both reap a store of happiness? Tell me, Miss Forsdyke, whether I am right in thinking that this proposal is agreeable to you ? Do you accept my offer ?'

He leans across her chair and takes her hand in his, in eager expectation of her reply. A low sigh issues from her lips, and she allows the fingers of her other hand to close nervously round his wrist, and then he hears her whisper an affirmative.

'Thank you,' he says, simply, and he raises her hand to his lips and seals his vow of friendship with a kiss.

She rises hurriedly from her seat, and stands before him, with her hand resting lightly on his shoulder.

'Mr. Grandby,' she says, speaking in quick, earnest tones, 'whether we are doing wrong or right, I cannot say. I can only tell you that I am happier at this moment than I have been for years. Everything seemed dark and black before you came, but now, by a few words from you, all is bright. I cannot thank you now sufficiently for what you have done, but I will do so another time. Ah! you have bestowed on me a priceless blessing—you have instilled into my heart a hope of future happiness. But it is getting late—I dare not stay here longer, or I shall be missed. Take me back to the ball-room, please, and oh! Mr. Grandby, be careful—be very careful! The thought of this friendship has given me a new life, and, if anything were now to prevent it, existence would become unendurable to me. Remember this, and do nothing rashly. Wait till you hear from me, for one false step on your part would ruin everything.'

She takes his proffered arm, and without a word they leave the secluded corner and walk along the balcony in the direction of the ball-room. The music is crashing forth the languishing strains of one of Waldteufel's masterpieces.

'Listen,' he says, 'do you know that valse? It is a good omen for the success of the great, platonic friendship.'

'Is it?' she whispers, tightening the pressure of her fingers on his arm; 'what, then, is its name?'

'*Toujours fidèle!*'

CHAPTER XI.

GRANDBY VIEWS THE SITUATION DOUBTFULLY.

DURING that period which elapses between dessert and bed-time, all things are apt to present themselves to mortal eyes in an atmosphere of *couleur-de-rose*. On the night of the dance, Frank Grandby retires to bed in an exalted state of happiness. Having carefully reviewed the situation under the soothing influence of a cigar, he has come to the conclusion that he has cause to consider himself one of the luckiest men on earth. That capricious jade, fortune, who has overlooked him for so many years, seems suddenly to have remembered his existence, and to have bestowed upon him one of her pleasing smiles.

This is how the case presents itself to him in that small hour of the morning.

He—a young man of a warm and affectionate disposition — has conceived the strongest interest in the personality of a strange young lady, who seems to him to be far from happy. Intuitively he is conscious of there existing between them a great affinity, and he determines to do his utmost to make her acquaintance, and to chivalrously offer himself in the character of a friend. And now comes the most delightful portion of the episode—for it appears that this same young lady has been inspired with exactly similar feelings with regard to himself. She, too, has similarly conceived a sudden interest in him, and has likewise resolved to ask him to be her friend. What could be more charming than such a state of affairs?

In the first place, her impulsive confidence has proved to him clearly that he was right in his belief that they were in a state of elective affinity to one another —and this is very gratifying to his mind, as a direct proof of the reliability of his intuition. And then, secondly, through her having met him half-way in his advances, all difficulties in the establishment of their friendship have been removed; and he finds himself suddenly in the position

of friend, adviser, and confidant to a young
and charming girl, who betrays by her
every word and gesture how fully she understands and appreciates the goodness of
his heart—which is a state of affairs most
gratifying to his self-esteem and vanity.

Yes—viewing the case in whatever light
he may, the matter appears to him one of
self-congratulation.   He has acquired a
friend—one who, in course of time, may
even take the place in his affections once
held by his dear dead sister—a friend
whose life is full of bitter sorrow—a friend
who looks towards him to shed brightness
on her existence.

'And I will do my very best,' he murmurs; 'I will strive my very utmost to
make her happy, poor little girl!' with
which worthy resolution, he turns out the
lamp, and rests his head on the pillow.

But in the cold, matter-of-fact hours of
the morning, when the brain awakes strong
and clear, after a long, refreshing sleep,
the alluring conceptions of the over-night
sometimes present themselves under totally
different aspects.   Grandby awakes to the
consciousness of a most uncomfortable

sensation, which certainly did not exist in his brain the night before.

He sits up in bed, and tries to analyse this feeling—and, after some mature consideration, he comes to the conclusion that there are certain points in his recently-established connection with Miss Forsdyke which hitherto he has overlooked. This is a most annoying discovery, but, being a young man with a rooted objection to groping in the dark, whatever may be the matter in hand, he resolves to view the whole case impartially and dispassionately, and to discover for himself exactly whether real cause exists for uneasiness of mind.

Now, at first sight, this seems a very easy thing to do, but, in the course of his mental analysis, he soon becomes conscious of the fact of his finding it extremely difficult to be either impartial or dispassionate in the matter in hand. Before the lapse of five minutes, he discovers that he is heavily biassed in one direction; and he feels that it will require arguments of the most weighty order to turn him aside from his fixed purpose of claiming the friendship which Miss Forsdyke has so generously offered him.

There are points in the case, however, which it is impossible to help noticing, and prominently amongst these stands the glaring unconventionality of the whole proceeding. Regarding it from whatever point he chooses, he cannot deny that the situation, from a social point of view, is peculiar and unique.

It is no good for him to argue that it is only the natural consequence of a young couple possessing mutual sympathies and kindred dispositions. The futility of such a line of argument is sufficiently obvious to prevent him from adopting it. He knows full well that the cold, conventional eye of society would not be likely to accept the existence of an elective affinity as an explanation of a breach of etiquette.

And, that he has committed a breach of etiquette, he no longer has a doubt. It requires no argument to convince him on that point. His common-sense tells him that to make the acquaintance of a young lady, to gain her confidence, to offer her his friendship, and to promise to do his utmost to make her happy in the future—all within the space of one short hour—is a

course of proceeding of a most extraordinary character, and one not generally
adopted in polite society.

But, having arrived at this point, he
suddenly drops the cautious, reflective
mood, and assumes a line of thought, the
independence of which is quite astonishing.

'Granting all this,' he says, 'wherein
lies the harm?'

Yes, that is the question. Admitting
that, according to existent conventional
regulations, the proceeding *is* irregular,
what possible harm can accrue therefrom?

Of course it is needless to say that,
having gone so far—having practically
removed an insuperable objection with a
mere inflection of the voice—he does not
take long to convince himself that to
attempt to withdraw from the connection
on the plea of etiquette would be to take
a mean advantage of which any gentleman
would be ashamed.

'Etiquette be hanged!' he murmurs, becoming quite excited. 'Of all the lying,
hypocritical humbugs of this world, social
etiquette is the worst. If a young man
and woman cannot form a friendship on
strict platonic lines, without getting into

difficulties, then—then I know nothing of the world;' from which remark the reader may probably conclude that his knowledge of the world was, in truth, limited.

Having thus satisfactorily settled the primary question under analysis—namely, the possibility of the existence of the proposed friendship—he now turns his thoughts towards another point which has been giving him some uneasiness of mind. The memory of her last few words are still lingering in his ears, and he repeats them over to himself.

'Wait till you hear from me. One false step on your part will ruin everything.'

To say the least of it, this is mysterious, and viewed in the unsentimental, early hours of the day there is a strong smack of the melodramatic about her caution. What could she have meant by her impressive injunction? Can there be any foundation for the uncomfortable suspicion which has fallen upon him that it is the young lady's intention to establish a friendship of a *clandestine* character?

The more he dwells upon the point, the more fully does he become convinced that he is right in his suspicion. He mentally reviews their conversation of the night before, and everything points to this conclusion. Her remarks as to the system of surveillance instituted over her every action; the vague hints which she has dropped regarding her aunt's mistrust; the hurried observation which she made on rising that if she stayed longer she would be missed, and various other indications pointing to the fact that she was not a free-agent in her uncle's house, all combine to make him think that it is not her intention to make her guardians party to the agreement.

This thought causes him grave anxiety. In offering his friendship to the girl the night before, such a course of proceeding as this had never entered his conception. He had merely imagined an intercourse, open and innocent, with no pretence to concealment or deception—an intercourse palpable to the whole world. It had been his intention to have called the next day on Colonel and Mrs. Renfrew, and to have been formally introduced to the girl in the presence of her relatives, thereby obtaining their tacit consent to his intimacy with their niece. But now a sudden conviction seizes him that such is not the course of proceeding expected of him by Miss Forsdyke. In proposing friendship to him, he feels assured that she has intended him to understand that it is to be of a secret character. In what other way can her parting words of 'Wait till you hear from me. One false step on your part will ruin all,' be construed?

According to this injunction, it is quite evident that his plan of calling on Mrs. Renfrew becomes impossible. Until Miss Forsdyke sends him word, he is to stir neither hand nor mouth, and therefore it is also evident that, as the matter stands, the projected friendship cannot progress. That Miss Forsdyke would not have thus enjoined him without some weighty reason on her part for doing so, he has no doubt, but what this reason can be, otherwise than that which he suspects, he is unable to conceive. If then it proves that he is right in his suspicion, the friendship will border closely on the regions of intrigue.

Now, to many young men of the present day, the possibility of an intrigue with a pretty girl would appear everything that is charming and delightful. But Frank

Grandby was of a different order of character. In all matters pertaining to the opposite sex, his chivalry bordered on the
quixotic. His belief in the instinctive
virtue and pure integrity of woman was
absolute, and he would have cut off his
right hand rather than have harmed, morally or in reputation, a trusting girl.

And so now, in great perplexity, he asks
himself the question, whether it would be
right and honourable for him to consent to
form a friendship with this young girl,
knowing that it was to be of a secret
character.

Holding the views he does, there can be
only one answer to the question, and that
is in the negative.

'No,' he says, 'it would be mean, un-
gentlemanly, and dishonourable. My
course of action is plain—I must distinctly refuse to be a party to the matter. It
may be that I am wrong in my conclusion;
after all, it is only conjecture that such is
her intention. Possibly in telling me to
wait she merely required of me a little patience, until she had sounded her relations
as to their concurrence in our plan. I
hope devoutly that such may be the case,

I am sure, for I am afraid that I shall cut
a very sorry figure, if I now back-out of
the agreement, after having been so ob-
trusively eager on the subject last night.
But, in spite of my earnest wish to be her
friend, there is no other course open to me,
if my suspicions prove correct. However,
it is no good thinking further on the matter, for until I hear from her it is impossible for me to know the true state of the
case. Probably I am erecting a mountain
out of the smallest of insignificant mole-
hills, so let's hope for the best, and—by
gad! it's nine o'clock—and I must be
thinking of getting up,' saying which,
Grandby throws off his clothes, and jumps
out of bed.

'Let's hope for the best,' he murmurs,
as he carefully shaves his chin, which
shows, it must be confessed, no striking
signs of hirsute manliness. 'Yes, by gad,
let's hope for the best!' and in another
moment he has divested himself of his
clothes and is splashing briskly amidst the
cold water of his morning tub.

CHAPTER XII.

LOFTUS MAKES A STATEMENT.

IT is ten before Grandby emerges from his
little house, and he walks rapidly down
the little sloping path leading towards the
hotel, feeling thoroughly ashamed of himself for being so late. He regrets not having followed up his performance of the
previous morning by a similar display of
energy ; but in palliation of his indolence
he reflects that last night's dissipation may
perhaps be taken as sufficient excuse for
the lateness of his appearance. But he
determines that it shall not occur again.
Such is his delight at finding himself in the
Himalayas, after two years broiling in the
plains, that he has fully made up his mind
to lose no opportunity of drinking in the
fresh mountain air.

On his right, some feet below him, lie

o 2

the tennis-courts of the hotel, but they bear a very gloomy, deserted aspect as he passes them. He rightly concludes that, after the excitement of the night before, the inmates of the hotel are not feeling in a specially athletic mood. In fact, with one or two exceptions, if the truth were known, they are all still in bed—but this of course he cannot know. In the eyes of the present highly-refined social world, it would be an act of the grossest impropriety for a young unmarried man to dare to contemplate directly or indirectly the possibility of female form ever being clothed in a *robe-de-chambre.*

Entering the breakfast-room he discovers one solitary individual, whom he has no difficulty whatever in recognising as Mrs. Lamb. She is looking more bilious and yellow than ever, and there is a worn, wearied expression on her haggard face, which does not enhance her natural charms. Not wishing particularly to have to undergo the infliction of a *tête-à-tête* repast, with a polite bow, he proceeds to pass onwards to the further end of the table. Her voice arrests him.

' Good morning, Mr. Grandby,' she says,

in a languid tone. 'Won't you come and sit nearer the fire? The morning air is very cold.'

'Thank you,' he says, courteously, 'you are very kind;' and he moves towards her, and, having taken his seat, orders breakfast. 'I trust, Mrs. Lamb,' he says, politely, feeling it incumbent on him to make some remark, 'that you are feeling none the worse for last night's entertainment.'

'No,' she says, in her thin voice. 'Well, perhaps I am feeling a little tired. But I make it a rule never to allow any gaiety to affect my usual routine, which accounts for my early appearance this morning. I think that it was a most enjoyable dance, don't you?'

'The little I saw of it seemed everything that a dance should be. But I left early. Being a perfect stranger here, I naturally did not find it so attractive as otherwise I might have done.'

'I am so sorry,' she says, in a tone of genuine sympathy, which takes him by surprise. 'Why did you not come to me? I would have introduced you to everybody. You must remember that here in the hills a ball-room presents a direct contrast to one in the plains; here the girls abound, and a man need never want a partner. Do you really mean to tell me that you did not obtain a single dance?'

'I can't say exactly that,' he says. 'Mr. Loftus introduced me to a young lady—a Miss Forsdyke, who is staying in this hotel,' he explains, in a tone of studied indifference, 'and she gave me one dance, so my card was not quite blank.'

'Ah!—Miss Forsdyke! And what do you think of her? They have not been here long, but they seem to be very retiring people, for as yet nobody seems to know them. She is a very pretty girl, I think, but she strikes me as being rather melancholy. Did you find her so?'

'Well, a first introduction dance,' he says, with a little laugh, 'does not offer many opportunities for discovering the peculiarities of one's partner's disposition. From what I saw of Miss Forsdyke, she seemed to be very similar to most young ladies. Perhaps, though, she was a little melancholy, now you come to mention it.'

'Ah! I thought so,' answers Mrs. Lamb. 'I have a suspicion that she does not agree very well with her uncle and aunt. They seem to be rather unpleasant people; though,' she adds, hastily, 'I have no right to pass an opinion on them, not knowing them. I believe her father is a colonel in the commissariat quartered at Sihayipur.'

'Sihayipur!' cries Grandby, in some surprise. 'Are you certain, Mrs. Lamb?'

'Well, I cannot say I am certain; but I fancy that I have heard that such is the case. But why do you seem surprised at the announcement?'

'Oh! nothing. Only that I have a very great friend in the Engineers, called Grafton, quartered there; and I was thinking that possibly she knew him.'

'Probably she does,' returns Mrs. Lamb, kindly. 'I conclude from the way you speak that he is a *very* great friend of yours. If so, it will be very nice for you to meet some one to talk to about him. I always envy you men your capability of forming great friendships with those of your own sex. That great pleasure is generally denied to us poor women. We are too vain and spiteful, and we are possessed of such jealous dispositions that a real friendship between us is almost an impossibility.'

'I am *no* judge of character,' thinks Grandby to himself. 'Mrs. Lamb appears to be a most estimable woman.'

He feels a positive liking towards her growing within him. The kindly way in which she has referred to his friendship with George Grafton has quite won his heart, and has caused him to change his preconceived ideas regarding her. In spite of her marked peculiarities she appears to be most amiable and well-disposed.

'Oh! you mustn't say that,' he says, with a little laugh; 'you will find in me a sturdy champion in the cause of woman's goodness.'

'It is very kind of you to say so,' she answers, rather sadly. 'But unfortunately age and experience tell me to the contrary. Think of the disgraceful scene enacted at this very table two nights ago! Can you conceive anything more vulgar and unlady-like? Do you believe that any two men would have forgotten themselves so far as to have descended to low abuse at a public dinner-table?'

'I really cannot say,' says Grandby, lamely, feeling rather embarrassed at this unexpected turn in the conversation. 'I suppose that it couldn't be helped.'

'Couldn't be helped! Of course it could have been helped. Had I had any sort of control over my unfortunate tongue, it would never have happened. But, unfortunately, Mr. Grandby, I am possessed of a villanous temper, and, before I know where I am, I am beside myself with rage. My temper is too powerful for my bodily strength, for I invariably end in tears,' and she gives a feeble smile.

'Well, you cannot say that you were not provoked?' says Grandby, sympathisingly.

'Yes, I was certainly provoked,' she says, closing her thin lips firmly together; 'but that is but a poor excuse for my reprehensible conduct. Had I acted rightly, I should have ignored the provocation. But really, with a quick temper like mine, I find it literally impossible to ignore Mrs. Stockton's gibes and covert sneers. She would provoke a saint. I can never meet the woman without experiencing a desire to do battle with her. It is very foolish of me, as I know that I have no chance against her, for she is literally invincible.'

'Well, anyhow, after you left the room she was worsted by Mrs. Renfrew.'

'So my husband told me, but I can hardly believe it. Mrs. Stockton's power of abuse is simply stupendous. But I can't tell you how ashamed I am of the part I took in the matter. It must have appeared so low and vulgar to outsiders.'

'It was very unfortunate, certainly,' says Grandby, feebly, feeling himself unable to say anything of a more consolatory character. 'But if you can't agree—I trust that you will excuse me making the suggestion —why don't you sit somewhere else, away from her? That would obviate all difficulties, and would prevent future disputes; and it would certainly be more pleasant to me;' and Grandby laughs good-humouredly.

'Ah! Mr. Grandby,' she says, 'I owe you a very humble apology for my conduct. I trust you will forgive me?'

'There is nothing to forgive, I can assure you,' he answers, earnestly. 'Pray don't let us refer to the matter further.'

'It is very kind of you to treat the matter so lightly. If you knew Mrs. Stockton as well as I do, you would perceive that, after all, there is some excuse for my behaviour. She is the most vindictive woman that I have ever met. When I first met her here in May, she even professed a friendship for me. But one day I annoyed her in some trifling matter, the nature of which I now forget, and she took offence, and since that day she has always behaved to me as she did the other night. She never forgives a slight—so take care, Mr. Grandby, how you behave towards her, or you may be getting into difficulties;' and Mrs. Lamb allows her pale face to light up into a faded smile.

'I am afraid your caution comes too late,' he replies, laughing heartily, 'for I am already in her bad books. Last night, at the dance, she as good as asked me to dance the lancers with her; and I refused point-blank with more promptitude than politeness.'

'Oh, dear me! did you really? Then I am afraid that she will give you trouble. She will never overlook a thing like that.'

'I caught her eye afterwards,' says Grandby, 'and she certainly looked a trifle venomous. I should say she was a magnificent hater.'

'You are quite right there,' assents Mrs. Lamb; 'I only hope that she won't annoy you, like she does me. If you can keep a check on your tongue you will be all right. But I need not have any doubt as to your self-control, for you are a *man*. And now I really must be going, so good-morning, Mr. Grandby. I hope that I shall have the pleasure of conversing with you again soon;' and she rises and languidly leaves the room, casting a glance of playful coquetry upon him as he stands holding the door open for her exit.

Grandby returns to the table and proceeds to finish his breakfast, which he eats with a great relish, the mountain air having already given him a glorious appetite. He muses over his late conversation with Mrs. Lamb, and comes to the conclusion that at heart she is a very nice woman. He is immensely surprised, too, at the discovery. Judging from what he had seen of her on the night of his arrival, he had conceived her to be a most unpleasing specimen of womanhood.

'It only proves,' he murmurs, 'that first impressions are not always infallible.'

The knowledge that, in all probability, Miss Forsdyke is acquainted with his friend, lends an additional attraction to the

already attractive scheme of forming a
platonic friendship with that young lady.
He reviews, in anticipation, the many con-
versations which they will hold in the discussion of Grafton and his belongings ; for
he has such a strong faith in the engaging
qualities of his friend, that he does not
doubt for one moment that Miss Forsdyke
will show otherwise than the keenest interest in the subject.

' Dear old George !' he murmurs to himself, affectionately, ' how nice it will be to
have some one to talk to about you—some
one who will readily sympathise with every
word I say concerning you.'

Having finished his breakfast, he takes
his hat and strolls down towards the post-
office.

' It is quite time to take some exercise,'
he says. ' Now that I am here I must
make the most of every moment.'

So he strolls leisurely along, walking
merely for walking's sake. Turning to the
right at the post-office he walks in the
direction of Tabernacle Point, one of the
extremities of the Doonga ridge. Everything is looking bright and charming. The
woods, the flowers, the cool, fresh air, the

glorious panorama, the songs of birds, the distant mountain peaks, as yet untinged with snow, all appeal directly to his senses, and make him glad.   Already, within only two days of his arrival, he has become another man.   He feels now so strong that he laughs amusedly at the recollection of his weary figure toiling miserably up the hill to Banbury's that day.   What a marvellous transformation has been effected within the last forty-eight hours, and how differently does life appear to him now to what it did then !

Occasionally he pauses as some striking natural effect presents itself to view.   He is an ardent admirer of nature, but never before has he beheld it on such a majestic scale, and, as he stands drinking-in with silent rapture the beauty of the scene, he becomes conscious of the fact that the Alps sink into insignificance before the grandeur of the Himalayas.   A troop of monkeys, crying and chattering in their undeveloped tongue, suddenly appear, and, with a mighty rush, leave their trees and scamper across the road.   In a moment, with incredible agility, they have mounted to the topmost branches of the trees, and, swift

as lightning, they pursue their course down
the hill. He watches them till they are
out of sight, and then he turns round and
retraces his steps. He has just remembered that he has promised to look up
Loftus that morning. So he steps bravely
out, feeling lighter in heart than he can
remember to have done since his arrival in
India two years before.

It is a little past one when he arrives
at the club, and he proceeds straight to
Loftus's room, and, to his surprise, he
finds that he is not in bed; but he shrewd-
ly guesses, after a moment's glance, that
the time his friend has been up is only a
question of minutes, for he is still un-
dressed.

Robed in a very handsomely-embroider-
ed Kashmir dressing-gown, with his feet
encased in a pair of soft, fur-lined slippers,
he is sitting in a low arm-chair beside a
blazing fire, in a state of languid indolence.
A cigar is in his mouth, and on a little
table at his hand is the inevitable decanter,
with a half-drained whisky-peg.

'How are you, old chap?' he says, lazily
extending his hand. 'Am deuced glad to
see you—take a seat there, will you?

And, if you want a peg, do you mind asking for it; it goes to my heart to be refused so often.'

'Well, Loftus,' laughs Grandby, sitting down, 'I am glad to see you looking so fresh and well. I must confess that I had expected to find you still in bed.'

'I have been up this ten minutes,' remarks Loftus, with a yawn. 'To tell you the truth, I became quite bored with lying in bed, so I got up; just for the sake of variety. It was very foolish of me to do so, for, without a sufficient quantity of sleep, a man cannot expect to get through his day's work.'

'You should do what I do. I was out of bed by nine, and, after a good breakfast, I went for a long walk, and the result is that I feel now as fresh and clear-headed as if I had gone to bed at ten o'clock last night.'

Loftus, slowly puffing at his cigar, stares at him for a couple of moments in contemplative silence.

'And did you meet her?' he says, presently.

'Meet her! Meet whom?'

'Oh! that's your game, is it? Well,

we will drop the subject, as you wish it. I have no desire to fathom your secrets.'

'But I can assure you that I don't understand you,' says Grandby, with a smile of amusement.

'Now, Grandby, look here,' says Loftus, impressively, laying down his cigar. 'It is no good your trying to take me in. As I have said before, I have no wish to force your confidence. If you want to keep silence on the matter, do so by all means, and I will ask no indiscreet questions. But if you fondly imagine that you can convince me that you went out for a walk with no ulterior object in view, beyond that of taking exercise, you will find yourself much mistaken. I am not half so young and innocent as I look, my boy. I know a thing or two, I flatter myself; and I know very well that young men in Doonga don't take long walks, unless there be a petticoat to break the dull monotony of the scenery.'

'But you are wrong, Loftus, I can assure you,' replies Grandby, laughing heartily. 'I went out for a walk merely for walking's sake.'

Loftus eyes him for a moment curiously.

'Say that again, please,' he says, slowly.

'I repeat that I went out for a walk merely for walking's sake.'

'Well, of course I must believe you,' says Loftus, reluctantly. 'But the whole thing beats me hollow. You are a rum cove, Grandby, really you are. You interest me—'pon my word you do; and I am very grateful to you for doing so, for there are not many things which interest me in this blooming world. I used to flatter myself that I knew something about life. But, the more I see of you, the more I become aware of how extremely limited is my vaunted knowledge. If you have no objection, old chap, I really must make a study of your character. A man who does not drink because he is not thirsty, and who takes a walk merely for walking's sake, is a creature past my comprehension. Yes—by all that's holy, I must really study you. I must buy a note-book, and perhaps in time I may begin to understand you. A man can master most difficulties by dint of application;' and Loftus revives his exhausted nature with a long draught from his high tumbler.

'We had a hell of a night last night,' he

remarks, reflectively, after a short pause. 'Why the deuce did you depart so early? I think on the whole that the dance was a success; but the late hour to which they continued dancing was very irritating. I can assure you that the last female did not turn out till past four o'clock. It is not only inconsiderate, but I hold that it is downright ill-bred. But women are proverbially selfish, so it was perhaps rather ridiculous to expect anything else of them. I have not the least doubt that ninety per cent. of the women here last night were of an opinion that their own sex is a necessary element to the success of a dance. Ridiculous, isn't it? 'Pon my word, it is a most laughable idea. And, what is more absurd, I don't believe that they would understand you if you told them to the contrary. If you took the trouble to explain to them that a dance was merely an excuse for a big night on a grand scale, they would probably think you mad. They would certainly call you a *liar* to your face, if Banbury's Hotel can be taken as a criterion of female manners. I shouldn't wonder if they don't imagine that the fun is over when the dancing finishes, instead

of just being on the point of beginning.
'Pon my life, women are rum fishes.   The
more I see of them, the more I wonder.'

'Extraordinary, aren't they?' says Grandby, gravely.   'But I daresay you made up
for lost time afterwards?'

'By gad, that we did just!' says Loftus,
his voice softening at the recollection. 'It
was the biggest thing I have ever known.
There wasn't a hitch in the whole proceeding.   One and all entered heart and soul
into the fun, and that fellow Bramley
made the wittiest speech I have ever
heard.   You *should* have seen him!   He
sat on the middle of the long table, with
the shell of the raised pie upon his head,
and he literally brought down the house—
at least, he did the table, for the leg broke,
and there was a mighty smash of crockery.
It was the grandest thing I have ever seen.
I split my dress-coat right across the back
with laughing so much, and then Pollock,
of the 10th, caught it by the tails, and
bang it went right up to the collar.   Champagne flowed in torrents,' he continues,
his eyes sparkling with excitement.   'Ah!
it was simply glorious.   The breakage of
glass, they tell me, beats all record, and I

can well believe it. How we ever got to
bed, I don't know; but I have a suspicion
that the servants rose to the occasion, and
lent a helping hand. I have a dim recollection of heaving my lamp at some nigger
after I was in bed, and that great pool of
oil on the floor there seems to corroborate
the notion, and then I suppose I fell
asleep, for I remember nothing further.
But what is the good of talking of it,' he
adds, in a regretful tone. ' It is all past
and gone. Every pleasure in this world is
evanescent.'

' Oh! come, cheer up; don't be down-
hearted,' laughs Grandby.

' How can I be otherwise ?' asks Loftus,
sadly. ' Look at me. Am I not a perfect
wreck? Have you ever seen anything
more truly pitiable in your life ? Is it not
monstrous to think that a human being
cannot enjoy himself on this third-rate
planet without suffering the next day
from splitting headache? Oh! I am a
perfect worm. And to think that it is all
past and gone, and that possibly months
may elapse before another such festive
night occurs. Ah! it is too horrible! But
let us change the subject,' he continues,

with a sigh. 'What did you think of your partner last night?'

'Of Miss Forsdyke?' asks Grandby, with well-simulated indifference. 'Oh! she seemed very nice.'

'Indeed! You thought her very nice, did you? Now such an epithet as that is hardly the one I should use in describing that young lady.'

'Why?' asks Grandby, in a tone of interest.

'Oh—well—I don't know,' answers Loftus, indifferently. '"Very nice" sounds rather tame when applied to a young lady of such peculiar powers of attraction as Miss Forsdyke.'

'Well, with regard to her peculiar powers of attraction, that of course is a matter of opinion. She did not strike me as being anything out of the common. She is pretty, certainly, in a mild way,' says Grandby, adopting a tone calmly critical; 'but then she can hardly be styled lively.'

'Oh! you think so, do you? Well, I can assure you that beneath that mask of melancholy there lies a fund of inexhaustable animal spirits. Oh! she can be lively enough, if she likes. Perhaps she was thinking over her past sins, and that made her feel rather sad last night.'

'I don't think that she leads a very happy life,' says Grandby, quietly.

'Why? What makes you think that?' asks Loftus, regarding him curiously from the corner of his eye.

'Well, from what she hinted, I conclude that Mrs. Renfrew is anything but kind to her.'

'Oh! she told you that, did she?' says Loftus, with a sarcastic smile. 'She seems to have been remarkably confiding during your twenty minutes' acquaintance. And what else did she tell you? I am distinctly curious to hear. Did she confide to you any of her hopes and aspirations for the future, and did she pray and implore you to grant her—just—a—*leetle* sympathy?'

'What nonsense you talk, Loftus!' says Grandby, shortly, feeling a trifle annoyed at his friend's mincing tones of mimicry. 'Our conversation, of course, was of the most commonplace nature. It was only indirectly that I came to the conclusion that her aunt was unkind to her.'

'Well—she is certainly a wonderful

young woman,' remarks Loftus, reflectively, leaning back and studying his cigar-ash. 'A little excitable, too, and apt at times to kick over the traces—if you will pardon me alluding indirectly to the young lady's legs. I should not be at all surprised if Mrs. Renfrew did not find a tight rein to be indispensable.'

'You talk as though you knew her well. May I ask where you have met her before?'

'I met her two or three years ago in Kashmir,' replies Loftus, slowly, still lost in admiration of the long white ash on his cigar. 'I met her there under—well, under rather peculiar circumstances, which gave me plenty of opportunity for studying her character; and I repeat that she is a very wonderful specimen of humanity. And you had better take care, Grandby, old chap,' he adds, in a chaffing tone; 'she is not the sort of woman to make a good wife.'

'That is rather a sweeping statement,' says Grandby, coldly. 'You certainly must have studied her character very deeply, if you feel justified in making such a broad assertion.'

'Hullo!' cries Loftus, starting up, 'don't excite yourself, old chap. I am sure I am

very sorry—I must apologise, but I really
had no idea that you had serious inten-
tions in that quarter. Perhaps the happy
day is already fixed? Don't forget to bid
your humble servant to the feast, and let
me implore you to get Heidsieck's very
best;' and he leans back and laughs
amusedly.

'What a fellow you are!' says Grandby,
trying vainly to stifle his annoyance. 'Let
us drop the subject. We have no earthly
right to take this young lady's name in
vain. I object to it on principle.'

'Oh, very well—certainly! I thoroughly agree with you on that point. Not that
we have really said anything to Miss Forsdyke's detriment. To be incapable of
making a good wife to a *poor* man—which
is, of *course*, what I meant—is nothing to
be ashamed of. It only signifies an ignor-
ance of the value of pounds, shillings, and
pence, and God knows that Miss Forsdyke
is not the only individual in the world ill-
informed on that all-important subject.
So kindly suggest another topic of conversation. Somehow, every subject to-day is
utterly nauseous to me.'

Grandby is very vexed with himself for

having shown annoyance at his friend's remarks. It was such an extremely foolish and unjustifiable proceeding on his part that he determines to remove any bad impression which his behaviour may have caused by laying himself out to be especially agreeable, and he so far succeeds in this object that, when he rises to go, Loftus, whose spirits have risen amazingly beneath his genial influence, becomes again plunged in the deepest melancholy at the thought of his departure.

'You are a brick, Grandby,' he says, enthusiastically. 'In spite of your peculiarities, you are the best companion that I have ever met. Mind you come in again. I shall probably be in this position for the next week, and I shall look forward anxiously to your appearance. So good-bye, old chap. There is the whisky and soda, if you want a peg. It would do my heart good to see you help yourself, but I shan't risk the chance of refusal by offering it to you. Good-bye. It is just two o'clock. Nine hours to bed-time. Oh, Lord, oh, Lord—was ever a man so cursed before?'

CHAPTER XIII.

LE PREMIER PAS.

GRANDBY is pleased to notice, as he enters the dining-room that night, that Mrs. Lamb has acted on his suggestion, and has changed places with her husband. She smiles a kindly good-evening to him as he takes his seat on her husband's right.

'You see what I have done,' she whispers to him behind the major's chair; 'I hope that I shall be quite safe here;' and she bestows on him a most languishing glance from out of her pale blue eyes. It is quite evident that Mrs. Lamb is by no means averse to having a handsome young man for her confidant.

The major laughs heartily at her remark.

'You are a wonderful diplomatist, my boy,' he says, turning to Grandby, 'I must make you my prime minister and confi-

dential adviser. With your assistance, we
should soon bring the war to an end.'

'Charles, how can you be so ridiculous?'
says his wife, with playful coquetry.

At this moment Mrs. Stockton enters,
and she takes in the situation at a glance.
With a loud snort of disapproval she seats
herself on Grandby's right. It is curious
to note the strange mixture of regret and
triumph depicted on her face as she contemplates the imperturbable form of Major
Lamb, effectually screening from view her
old opponent. She cannot conceal her delight at recognising Mrs. Lamb's tacit
acknowledgment of defeat, but, having
employed the day in the study of new and
startling methods of attack, she naturally
feels disappointed at finding herself unable
to display them in the arena.

Grandby, paying no heed to her spasmodic grunts, turns his back on her, and
engages in conversation with the major.

'In my young days,' she says, addressing no one in particular, 'it was considered
bad manners to turn one's back upon a
lady.'

'I beg your pardon,' says Grandby, coldly, turning quickly round with a slight

flush upon his face, ' I was unaware that
you wished to address me, Mrs. Stockton.'

' And more I do,' she says, sharply.
' Pray don't let me interrupt your conversation with Major Lamb. It must, I am
sure, be of a highly edifying character.'

Without a word Grandby turns away,
and addresses Major Lamb. Not in the
least disconcerted by the suddenness of
her attack, he resumes the conversation at
the point where it was arrested by her
first remark. She notices his calm indifference, and grows palpably redder in the
face.

' H'm !' she ejaculates, ' how very polite !'
and she turns her attention for the moment to her food.

' And so poor Miss Forsdyke is not well,'
she says, after a short silence, still addressing vacancy : ' Confined to her room with a
sore throat ! I really do not wonder at it,
though, after sitting out on that balcony
as she did last night. It showed a great
want of judgment on the part of her partner—but then perhaps *he did not dance the
lancers,*' she adds, with an unmistakable
sneer.

No one answers her, or pays the least

attention to her remark. The residents of
Banbury's Hotel know the woman too
well to dare to enter into a conversation
with her when she is in one of her aggressive moods. The most ordinary observation would be seized upon as an excuse for
an attack.

Grandby, unable to prevent the hot
blood from mounting to his face as he
hears the inuendo, applies himself more
than ever to his conversation with the
major, and the latter, guessing how the
matter stands, talks incessantly, commenc-
ing the narration of a long anecdote,
which occupies their attention for the next
ten minutes.

Mrs. Lamb in vain tries to stifle her
excitement. The old longing to be ' up
and at them ' cannot be repressed, and her
husband has to turn round more than once
to whisper a hasty caution in her ear.

The dinner progresses slowly. Mrs.
Stockton at intervals addresses space, but
her covert sneers and inuendoes fall point-
less on her listeners' ears, though Grandby
understands them. He comprehends now
that he has indeed made a relentless enemy
of the woman. The thought does not,

however, occasion him much uneasiness of
mind, for he has a complete faith in his
own self-control, and nothing that she says
will have the power to induce him to accept the challenge. His calm contempt
galls her to the quick, and she redoubles
her exertions. Once he commits himself
to a retort, she feels that the victory will
be hers !

But he never does commit himself ! He
receives her gibes and sneers with the most
aggravating indifference, and gradually
she ceases in her attack, and relapses into
moody silence.

It is a great relief to him when the meal
comes to an end. Do what he may, it is
impossible for him to repress the annoyance which he feels with regard to Mrs.
Stockton's unwarrantable attack. He rises
with the ladies and leaves the room.

'Oh, Mr. Grandby, how I admire you !
How I envy you your coolness,' whispers
Mrs. Lamb, in tones of open rapture, as
she passes him in the hall.

He gives a feeble smile, but says nothing,
and in another moment he is striding savagely up to his own house.

The small charcoal fire is burning brightly as he enters. He walks to the table and turns up the lamp, and immediately his anger evaporates, for he sees lying before him on the table a little three-cornered note, similar in character to the one which he received the night before. He hastily tears it open and reads it.

'DEAR MR. GRANDBY,

'I feel that I owe you an explanation. We separated so abruptly last night that I quite forgot to agree upon a plan of action. I have much to tell you and to discuss—you see, I already regard you as my best of friends. Do you know the little sheltered wood on the left of the road above the telegraph office? Take the footpath past the Banbury lawn-tennis courts, and lead straight on up the avenue till you come out into the open, when the road takes a semi-circular sweep round the side of the hill. The wood is on your left, by a partially-concealed little pathway, winding down the hill. You cannot fail to mistake it. Meet me there to-morrow at four o'clock, and I will tell you everything, which my emotion last night prevented me from doing. Ah! Mr.

Grandby, how can I ever thank you for your kindness? Already I feel a different being.

'From your very sincere friend,

'D. F.'

Twice he reads the letter through from beginning to end, and then he lights a cigar, and draws the arm-chair closer to the stove, and he sits down and begins to think.

What is he to do? That is the question which requires an immediate answer. Is he to meet the girl at the time appointed, or is he not? Shall he voluntarily make himself a party to the intrigue, or shall he refuse, writing a few lines in explanation of his conduct? His head is very cool and clear, and he views the question in its every aspect. One thing is now evident——it is Miss Forsdyke's intention that their intimacy shall be of a clandestine character. After carefully studying the letter, and analysing the feelings which prompted the writer to pen each phrase, he can arrive at no other signification of her meaning. And he does not judge her too hastily on this point. For the sake of argument, he tries to imagine that such is not the young lady's intention—that she, in fact, intends their intercourse to be open and apparent to the world, but that for the time being the character of their projected intimacy will have to be modified on account of some unknown circumstance, which will be explained to him on the morrow, when they meet.

This is a very pleasing explanation, and if accepted, without further analysis, as the truth, it opens out an easy channel of escape from a most unpleasant dilemma. But Frank Grandby's nature is too honest to attempt to deceive himself with such a shallow piece of sophistry. His common-sense at once tells him that such an explanation is fallacious, and he rejects it; for, if such had been her intention, in writing to him she would have mentioned the fact, apologising for the necessity of such an unconventional course of proceeding.

But in her letter there can be found no reference to the subject, and it has evidently been written with care and thought, and the omission of such an important reference cannot be explained on the score of forgetfulness or haste. No, it is evident she has written it with the fixed idea that their intimacy is to be formed on secret lines, and also on the understanding that he, too, is a party to the agreement.

This last consideration gives him much perplexity. If Miss Forsdyke be labouring under the mistaken idea that he has understood from the beginning that her offer of friendship was intended to signify a clandestine intimacy, he feels that he is in a very awkward situation, and also that it will be an extremely unpleasant duty on his part to undeceive her on this point; and that such is her idea he now feels thoroughly convinced, though for what reason she has become possessed of it he cannot conceive.

He tries to recall their conversation of the night before, thinking that possibly, by his own words, he may have led her to imagine that such was her intention. But in this he fails; he can only remember the substance, and not the exact wording, which he used. He can see her again as he saw her then, sitting in the soft moonlight, pale, tearful, and superbly lovely, and he can hear again her sweet low voice, choked with emotion, giving vent to the passionate utterances of a broken spirit, throwing, in her distress, conventional modesty to the winds, and imploring him, a stranger, to take pity on her loneliness, and to grant her sympathy.

Such a picture as this cannot fail to touch the tender sensibilities of a susceptible young man, and Grandby gives himself up wholly to the reminiscence, musing, half sadly, half fondly, over every detail. What unhappiness is hers! How childlike and confiding are her ways!—how passionately she yearns for a loving friendship, built on the solid rock of mutual sympathy!—how sad and inscrutable that a young girl of her physical and mental attractions should be doomed to a life of misery and pain!

The moments pass, the coke fire burns low, the lamp flickers and gives signs of a waning life, and still he remains with his thoughts concentrated on the great question occupying his mind. Shall he go, or shall he not? Shall he write to her and reject her proffered friendship, or shall he accept it as it stands, and meet her on the morrow at the place appointed? Shall he wilfully destroy all her new-born hopes of future happiness? Shall he allow a con-

ventional prejudice to overcome his desire
to shed brightness on her life ?

It is a question not to be answered hurriedly. To him it appears a question of
overpowering gravity. He knows that it
is in his power to help a fellow-creature,
and the question resolves itself into a
question of right and wrong—into the question whether, possessing the power, it would
be right for him to refuse to avail himself
of it. And his heart pulls one way, and
the deadly influence of conventionality the
other, each one predominating in its turn,
only to be again overcome by the other.

Which is he to do ? Which is the right
path for him to take ?

It becomes a struggle between the heart
and conscience ; for what is called conscience in these days is merely the reflection of ideas as to right and wrong, formed
by the overbearing arrogance of a dogmatic
conventionality.

And so through the small hours of the
night the struggle continues, till he becomes faint and weary with sophistical
arguments and ceaseless reiteration.

At last he rises. Unable to choose between the two sides of the question, he

has weakly compromised, and has determined to take a middle course.

'I will meet her to-morrow,' he murmurs, taking off his coat. 'I will meet her, and then explain to her personally my. objections on the subject. This will be the most gentlemanly way of telling her of her mistake. Would to God I had more resolution—and—and—would to God I were not so bound down by the rules of social conventionality.'

CHAPTER XIV.

THE AUTHOR CONTROVERTS A BASE SUSPICION.

HAVING once made up his mind upon the matter, Grandby deems it advisable not to discuss the question further. His mind is so torn between alternate decision and indecision, that he feels convinced that no amount of argument will bring him to a satisfactory solution of the problem. So he accepts as final his determination of the night before, and he does his best during the next day to avoid thinking on the matter.

To some his conduct may appear high-flown and verging on the ridiculous. Goodness gracious! I hear them say, what, in the name of fortune, is the man making such a fuss about? Here is a young and lovely maiden, forlorn and friendless, imploring him to give her his friendship, with the assurance that he, by so doing, will make her sombre existence bright and happy! What could be more charming, more self-gratifying than this? Is he incapable of appreciating his extraordinary good fortune in thus having a young lady deliberately throwing herself into his arms? Does not the knowledge that his external person has created a deep impression in the heart of a beautiful girl have a soothing effect on his *amour propre?* Is not his vanity tickled by the circumstance?

If not—if he be totally unconscious of the honour which the lady has vouchsafed to him—then he is, to say the least of it, a boor, a man utterly wanting in refinement, a lout, a creature not worthy of a woman's thought. Or is he pious? Is he that most detestable of human beings, a masculine prude? Does he shrink from the young lady's summons, because it would be a *naughty* thing to do?

If so, then send him back to the nursery! Let him study orthodox theology, and take orders, and become a snivelling curate, and give up his life to the joint duty of propagating the Gospel and the species! *We* do not want to be troubled with reading of such a limp, uninteresting specimen of humanity! Give us something with plenty of backbone, something strong and manly, with a character rising superior to the milk-and-water qualities requisite for a deaconship! Give us something dashing, with a *soupçon* of naughtiness, to remove all chance of insipidity—something we can admire and criticise reprovingly! That is what we want, and not a creature who refuses to meet a charming young girl, because, according to his wretched code of morality, it would be a very wicked thing to do. Who ever heard of such a despicable character attempting to pose as the hero of a novel? If this be the plain, unvarnished truth, we close the book, and refuse to read another word. We are no tyros in the art of novel-reading, and we know to a nicety what to expect for our money, and we are determined to get our money's worth, and not to be imposed upon by such a palpable second-rate article!

Gentle reader, I hasten to set your doubts at rest. Frank Grandby is neither boor nor prude. Such an epithet as the former could not possibly be applied with any justice to a man of his natural grace of form and manner. 'To look at him was to love him,' a young lady once remarked to her bosom-friend, in the strictest confidence, in the privacy of her chamber; and the author is in a position to vouch for the truth of this tender avowal from the bosom-friend in question, having come the next day, and repeated it to him *verbatim—also* in the strictest confidence.

So disabuse your mind at once of this idea. And as to the other point—as to whether Grandby justly deserves the epithet of prude—the author does not require the intermediary assistance of a third party to enable him to give an unqualified denial to the accusation, for he is in a position to vouch to the contrary from his own personal experiences.

No, rest assured, dear reader, my hero is no saint, but on the other hand he is no libertine. His character strikes a happy medium between profligacy and sanctity. It has in its composition none of the gross sensualism of the reprobate, and none of the canting humbug so inseparable in these days from the idea of piety. It is pure and honourable, unselfish and refined, and

in all matters pertaining to womankind
rising to the truly noble.

His one reason for hesitation with regard
to Miss Forsdyke's proposal was the fear lest
he, in complying with her request, should
do her harm both in her own eyes and in
the eyes of the world. As he estimated the
situation, she was acting under a sudden
impulse. Borne down with the weight of
her private sorrows, and hungering for a
kind word, in a moment of thoughtlessness
she had thrown conventionality to the
winds, and had written him the letter. That
she would repent of this error of judgment
on her part, when she became calm enough
to view the matter dispassionately, he did
not doubt. An awakening would come to
her—and would come to her perhaps too late.
If he were to obey her request implicitly, and
consent to form a secret friendship with her
then, at a time when her mind was clouded
by pain and suffering, what would be her
feelings, when she at last awoke to the
reality of the situation ? In what light
would she regard him for having so eagerly
acceded to a request made at a moment
when she was incapable of thinking right-

ly? Would she not scorn and loathe him, and would she not scorn and loathe far more her own self-degradation? This was how he argued; this was the picture which his imagination pourtrayed, thus unconsciously excusing and exonerating her for the questionableness of her behaviour.

Ninety men out of a hundred would have regarded the matter in the light of an agreeable escapade, and would have seized eagerly on the possible pleasures and excitements which might accrue from it; not actuated by any base sensual motives, be it understood, but merely by a thoughtless love of intrigue and adventure. But Grandby was different. From the moment that he viewed the matter calmly, and saw that it was not merely a question of personal desire, but one concerning possibly the honour and good name of an innocent young girl, it became to him a question of overpowering gravity, and he resolutely determined to stifle the promptings of his heart, and to obey the dictates of his conscience.

So, firm in this resolve, he might have been seen between the hours of three and four wending his way towards the place of assignation. There was a look of intense preoccupation on his face, as he left behind him the garden of the hotel, and entered on the broad road leading up the hill. To his sensitive disposition his present position was peculiarly embarrassing. He knew well how eagerly Miss Forsdyke had set her heart upon the fulfilment of the scheme, and he could not conceal from himself that he, quite unconsciously on his part, must have led her to understand that he too was a willing participant in it—and the knowledge that it devolves on him now to rudely dispel her illusion is painful to him in the extreme. But he does not waver in his determination; it is his duty to reject the friendship on the lines proposed, and he nerves himself to the unpleasant task before him. That he will succeed he has no doubt; but to ensure success he is conscious that he will have to cause her pain, and his tender heart shrinks from the idea.

It is a glorious autumnal afternoon. A faint breeze is lightly rustling the heavy foliage, which from either side of the road forms a leafy covering overhead, and patches of warm sunlight penetrating through this natural sun-shade fall here and there, bathing in gold the dark-green ferns and yellow balsam. The air, soft and warm, is redolent of deodar and pine, and Grandby, as he steadily pursues his way, drinks in long refreshing draughts invigorating both to mind and body. It is impossible to resist the soothing influence of this soft August afternoon, and gradually his uneasiness subsides, and he becomes less disquieted.

Arriving at the end of the long avenue, he emerges into the open. On his right stretches for miles and miles the splendid mountain scenery, growing dim and grey in the far, far distance. On his left rises a rugged mass of rock, jutting out from the summit of the hill, like some fierce promontory on the coast. At this point a little footpath branches off from the main road, and encircles round this bold projection. Lying almost concealed from view by the jagged wall of stone, it leads down the hill, through the sombre shades of a sheltered wood—and it leads towards the spot of assignation. He cannot restrain the beatings of his heart as he lightly treads the bridle-path, but, though he anxiously glances into the recesses of the rapidly thickening wood, no waiting, expectant figure meets his eye.

The thought strikes him that possibly he may be before his time, so he looks at his watch, and discovers that he is late, instead of being early. So he hastily pursues his way, looking carefully to the right and left, hoping and yet fearing to see the winsome form of Miss Diana Forsdyke. Following the serpentine windings of the little path which gradually descends the hill, he soon loses sight completely of the road above. The thick wood through which he now wends his way is hushed in a solemn silence; not a sound breaks the stillness of the air, save the cracking of the twigs and leaves beneath his feet. In a few moments he has seemingly stepped from the busy world of life into a shady glen, untrammelled by the bonds of human influence—a glen where Nature reigned supreme, unquestioned.

No spot on the whole of the Doonga Range could have been chosen more suitably for their meeting-place; and he notices the fact, and experiences a sense of thankfulness in consequence. He sees at

once that there is but small chance of
their meeting being observed in these dark
glades.

He has penetrated down into the deep
recesses of the wood for over a quarter-of-
a-mile before he comes across the object
of his search.   Walking along, half in
doubt as to whether he has not mistaken
her directions, a sudden turning of the
path brings her into view.   The close
undergrowth which has hitherto lined the
pathway on either side has disappeared,
and he sees before him a broad stretch of
fern and yellow balsam, waving gently
in the breeze, in the midst of which,
emerging like an island from the sea, rises
a giant oak, surrounded at the base by a
gently undulating knoll of soft green turf.
And it is on this fairy hillock, with her
back leaning against the tree, that he sees
Miss Forsdyke.

She does not see him at first, for her
eyes are directed to the ground, on which
she is mechanically tracing figures with
her parasol, so he has good opportunity of
scanning her *petite* form.   She is dressed
in a tailor-made costume of dark brown
cloth which fits her like a glove, and a veil

of a similar colour is wound around the small felt hat which crowns her auburn hair. Upon her witching countenance rests an expression of undisguised anxiety, which however rapidly disappears, giving place to one of joy, as she suddenly looks up and sees him quickly advancing in her direction. She makes a hurried step towards him, and in another moment her hands are resting lightly on his arm, and she is looking up into his face with a smile of child-like confidence.

CHAPTER XV.

AMICUS VITÆ SOLATIUM.

'You have come!' she says, in a quick, eager voice, 'you have come at last. I was so frightened, lest something had prevented you.'

He looks down into the lovely upturned face, and sighs. He is thinking how hard it will be for him to tell her of his resolve.

'Oh, Mr. Grandby,' she says, with a little laugh, 'you really must not sigh like that. Consider how very uncomplimentary it is to me. What is the matter? Are you tired? I am afraid that you are not strong enough to walk so far;' and she scans his face with a look of anxious inquiry which thrills him to the bone.

'Yes, Miss Forsdyke, I have come,' he says, in an embarrassed tone, 'I have come because you commanded me to do so—but

I have come against my will. At the club, two nights ago, we were very agitated, and we must have misunderstood one another. In proposing to you this friendship I had never intended that it should be of a secret character. I do not wish to cause you pain. God knows how sincerely I wish, as far as it lies in my power, to make you happy. Will you hear me patiently for a moment? I received your note last night, asking me to meet you here to-day. It was not until I had read it through that it struck me that possibly we had misunderstood one another at the club. It was my wish then, and it is my earnest wish now, to be allowed to call myself your friend; but it never entered my mind that the friendship which we agreed to form should be of a character such as your note insinuated. Tell me, Miss Forsdyke, am I right in my conjecture that it is your intention to keep our intimacy a secret from your guardian and the world? If I am wrong—if you will tell me that I have arrived at a false conclusion—a great weight will be lifted off my mind, and I owe you the most humble of apologies.'

He looks anxiously down at the little

R 2

figure by his side. Her head is averted from his gaze, so he cannot see the expression on her face, but he observes that her hands are clasped nervously together, as though she were a prey to some emotion. He pauses for a moment, awaiting her answer, but she makes no reply.

'Tell me,' he says, softly, 'am I right or wrong?'

She half turns her face towards him, and he sees that it is deadly pale.

'Why don't you say at once, Mr. Grandby,' she says, in a quivering voice, 'that you despise me?'

'Your inner conscience must tell you that your reproach is unjust,' he answers, gently. 'I sympathise with you far too deeply to be capable of entertaining the feeling which you suggest. In reality, I am a stranger to you; but, such is the strength of my sympathy, that I feel that I have known you all my life. I see you unhappy—I wish to do my best to make you happy; I find you friendless—I wish to be your friend. But I wish above all things to act towards you honourably—to know you with the full consent of Mrs.

Renfrew—and not to meet you here, in the sheltered recesses of a wood, out of sight of all mankind.'

She turns towards him with her large blue eyes filled with anxious wonderment.

'I do not understand you,' she says, in a frightened sort of whisper. 'Why should we not meet here together, out of sight of all mankind? What do you mean by acting honourably towards me? How could you act otherwise than honourably? Are you afraid of doing me some injury? Oh! Mr. Grandby, tell me what you mean! You are not joking, are you, just to frighten me? You really are in earnest, are you not?'

How can he tell her what he means? He looks into her childlike face, gazing up at him with an expression of bewildered innocence, and he sighs again, for he feels that the task before him is very hard. He had never imagined for one moment that she would be actually unconscious of the gross impropriety of her proposed plan of intercourse.

'If you cannot understand me from what I have just said,' he says, 'it will be very difficult for me to make my meaning

plainer. You are a girl, young and innocent, and you know nothing of the evils of
the great world in which you live. You
are perhaps ignorant even of the existence
of the thousand tongues of scandal which
are lurking here and everywhere, like
beasts of prey, awaiting their opportunity
to destroy. But believe me, dear Miss
Forsdyke, they do exist. They are present
everywhere, in every community, great and
small—ever on the watch to detect some
breach of etiquette—some departure, however trifling, from the conventionalism of
the social world. And, when they are
successful in their search, they show no
mercy. It is a horrible contemplation to
see men and women, outwardly professing
the Christian faith, gloating like filthy
carrion-birds over the mutilated carcase of
a fellow-creature ! They never spare, they
publish abroad, exaggerating and embel-
lishing, according to their fiendish fancy ;
they tear to pieces everything that is good
and pure, rejecting all extenuating circumstances and explanations; with bigoted
fury and diabolical injustice they pursue
their victim to the end, never resting until
they have divested him or her, as the case

may be, of every particle of claim to honour and good name; and then when all is over —when the carcase lies quivering at their feet—they raise their eyes to heaven and thank their God that they are not as other men. Do you understand me now?'

A shiver runs through her frame and a slight flush illuminates her dead-pale cheek as she bites nervously at her lower lip. Her eyes are directed to the ground, and for some moments there is silence. Then she suddenly raises her face and speaks.

'Yes—I understand you now,' she murmurs, sadly. 'You mean that the hateful world would attribute wicked motives to me if I were to meet you here in private. That is what you mean, is it not?'

'I insinuated that such might be the case, Miss Forsdyke,' he answers, in an embarrassed tone. 'Do you not see how scandal-mongers, would seize on the opportunity of blasting our characters, if we were to be seen walking here together? Even now I tremble at the risk which you are running. To me—a man—it is but of small importance; but to you—a woman— it is a question of life and death.'

'You frighten me with your vehemence,'

she whispers, placing her hand upon his arm. 'But there is no need, really, for you to be afraid for me. This wood is never visited—I know it well. When I was last in Doonga, I spent many, many lonely hours here, day after day, and I never saw a human soul. It is quite deserted—that little path leads nowhere, and is never used.'

She speaks with a suppressed eagerness which takes him by surprise. It seems as though, even now, she did not comprehend the gravity of the situation.

' Ah! Miss Forsdyke,' he answers, quickly, 'you do not understand me quite. This wood may be quite deserted, but still there always is the chance that some one may pass through it. Why should we run this terrible risk, when we could live in perfect friendship without infringing social laws? What reason is there for this clandestine arrangement? Allow me to take the matter into my own hands, and arrange it in the proper way: I will call to-morrow on Mrs. Renfrew, and will be formally introduced to you by her. Then, afterwards, we can meet before the whole world, without fear of censure.'

She turns away from him with a weary movement, and leans her arms upon a projecting bough.

'It is you, not I, that do not understand,' she murmurs. 'Do you think, if such a proceeding as you propose were practicable, that I should ever have had recourse to different means? You cannot grasp my forlorn position. You talk as though nothing were easier than to effect what you propose. You know nothing of the peculiarity of my surroundings; you do not understand my strange existence. And why should you? How could you be expected to know details concerning a—perfect—stranger?'

There is a ring of sadness in her tones which touches him to the heart. A yearning comes across him to seize her by the hand and to tell her of his devotion to her cause. But, before he can speak, she turns towards him with a passionate gesture.

'Leave me—leave me, Mr. Grandby!' she cries. 'It was but a dream which can never be fulfilled. I was foolish—mad to build my hopes on such a fanciful chimera. Go, Mr. Grandby—it can never be! You are right in all you say, and I am wicked to try to argue otherwise. But I cannot help myself—my disappointment is greater than I can bear. Ah! if you would only understand what I lose in giving up your friendship! To you the world is soft and smiling; to me harsh, antagonistic, unsympathetic, brutal. I had fancied that perhaps my loveless life would have grown a little brighter in the next few weeks. But what is the good of fancying, wishing, praying, hoping in this dreary world—it is all blank misery and despair.'

In another moment she is leaning against the tree, her form trembling with suppressed weeping. Moved to the quick, he takes a step towards her, and places his hand upon her shoulder.

'Miss Forsdyke,' he says, and his voice is quivering with emotion, ' pray compose yourself—I cannot bear to see you so distressed. Try to think of me as a fond and faithful friend, whose one desire in life is to make you happy. Instead of telling me to go away, confide in me, and let me understand why my project is unfeasible. I know that you are unhappy—I know that your tender heart is bruised and scarred by harshness and unkindness from those whose duty it is to love and cherish you. Cannot you tell me more? I do not wish to force your confidence, but I wish to be your friend—and if you would only deign to look on me as such, and tell me the particulars of your sad position, perhaps together we might find some method of bringing about that friendship which now you deem impossible.'

' But it cannot be otherwise than impossible,' she answers, sadly, without turning her face towards him.

' Only tell me why,' he says, in a pleading tone. ' It may not seem impossible to me.'

' How can I make you understand?' she says, in a weary voice, slowly wiping her eyes with a dainty little pocket-handkerchief. ' To me it seems as clear as day, but to attempt to explain it to you is far beyond my powers.'

' Ah! try,' he says, eagerly. ' Make an effort. Remember the subtle bond of sympathy which exists between us. How can you imagine that I shall fail to understand when every word you speak, every sigh you breathe, every laugh which issues from your mouth, finds a kindred echo in my heart?'

'Oh, Mr. Grandby,' she says, and her voice is full of a grateful softness. 'When you speak to me like that, I seem to become a different being—the whole world appears to change—the darkness vanishes, and my heart is filled with a sense of peacefulness. I often think,' she continues, wistfully gazing into the depth of foliage above her head, 'that possibly it may be my own fault that I am not happy. If I could only be as other girls, if I could only think and act as other girls—seeing only the brighter side of things—extracting only joy and happiness from their surroundings, and refusing to see all that is dark and gloomy —feeling no vague yearnings after impossible ideals and never experiencing the want of sympathy. If I could only be as they—why should I not be happy too? But I am strange—my nature is peculiar— I cannot find enjoyment in a loveless world. What are pleasures, joys, gladness, without love? How can one be happy without sympathy?'

'There is nothing strange in what you

feel,' he says, resting his arm on the bough
and turning towards her half-averted
figure. 'Do not I tell you that I feel the
same ? Without the existence of love or
sympathy, the idea of perfect happiness
becomes impossible to me. I fully comprehend your meaning, Fate has placed
you in an antagonistic world, against the
jarrings of which you are not strong enough
to stand. Your tender sensibility is unable
to brave the cheerless aspect of your surroundings. They do not understand your
nature—it is an inscrutable mystery to them.
They assign harsh, prosaic motives to your
every word and action. They deem you
strange and unconventional because your
soul is capable of a refined susceptibility,
which they cannot understand. Am I not
rightly describing your existence ?'

'You read me like a book,' she says,
lifting her face, and looking straight into
his eyes with a smile of ineffable sadness on
her lips. 'That subtle chord of sympathy,
which exists between us two, gives you
power to divine the inmost secrets of my
heart. As you speak, hope seems to rise
within my breast—a vain, transcendental
hope, which can never be fulfilled. Oh !

that I could possess your friendship! Oh! that I could call you friend, if only for a month, a week, a day! That would indeed be happiness.'

She leaves the tree, and stands before him with her hands clasped in an attitude of passionate entreaty. In her agitation, her whole frame seems transfigured—electrified into a more than earthly beauty. How can he resist her? How can he look upon that lovely face unmoved? How can he listen to those pleading tones, without the warm blood of youth coursing tumultuously through his veins?

He takes a hurried step towards her, and seizes her by both her hands.

'Miss Forsdyke,' he cries, ' you are right, and I am wrong. We must be friends—it is so ordained above. No conventional prejudice can step between us two. You say that, otherwise than in this secret way, it is impossible for us to form a friendship. I do not ask you the reason why—I implicitly believe you, and am ready to obey you.'

'How can I thank you for your noble words?' she cries, gratefully, with a trace of moisture in her eye. 'You have made me so happy that I hardly dare to speak— I hardly dare believe that it is true—that I have found a friend at last—a real friend, who will intuitively understand me, and sympathise with all my sorrows. But oh! Mr. Grandby, it goes to my heart to think that our meeting here in this way is not agreeable to you. But it cannot be altered. You do not know my aunt—she would never countenance an intimacy between us—she would probably never let us speak. I am never allowed to converse with any stranger—man or woman—unless it be in her presence. She follows me with her eyes and watches my every word and action. I have no peace—no freedom— she treats me like a slave—and sometimes I wish that I were dead.'

'But why does she act in this brutal manner?' he asks, his breast heaving with indignation. 'Can you assign no reason for her behaviour? Why does not your father interfere?'

A vivid blush sweeps across her face and neck, and she turns away her eyes from his look of searching inquiry. For a moment there is perfect silence ; then suddenly she speaks, her eyes suffused with tears.

'It is by my father's strict injunction that she behaves like this. She, herself, is not to blame.'

'What !' he says, in tones of amazement. 'Your father . . . .'

'Yes, my own father,' she cries, interrupting with an impassioned emphasis. ' My father—my own flesh and blood—the only human creature I have to love ! He it is, who makes my life what it is, who enjoins my aunt to keep a strict surveillance over me, to spy my every action. He it is, to whom I owe my great unhappiness. And I could love him—I could love him— oh ! so dearly, so passionately, if I were allowed to do so, if my every overture towards affection were not met by a maddening indifference—a heartbreaking chilliness of manner. He does not understand me— no one understands me in this dreary world. It seems to be my fate to be misunderstood by one and all mankind.'

'You forget our vow of friendship,' he says, in a reproachful voice. 'Henceforth you may rest assured there will be one person who thoroughly understands you.

What you tell me regarding your father
pains me to the quick. What is the reason
for his harshness?'

Again the vivid flush of scarlet suffuses
her neck and cheeks. A look of the
deepest embarrassment settles on her face,
accompanied by a nervous twitching of the
lips. It seems as though she were attempting to speak, but no sound comes to break
the stillness of the darkening wood. Only
a faint breeze, harbinger of the coming
night, can be heard gently rustling midst
the pines.

'Do not tell me if it gives you pain,' he
says, gently, taking her hand in his.

' But I will tell you,' she says, in a faint
whisper. 'If we are to be friends, I must
hide nothing from you. The reason of my
father's harshness is that—that he does not
trust me.' Her voice sinks so low that he
can barely hear her words. He stands
there, holding her by the hand, gazing intently into her half-averted face, and trying
to comprehend her meaning. She does not
attempt to look him in the face. He can
see, in the deepening twilight, that she is
shrinking sensitively away from him, and
he feels her vainly attempting to free her

hand from his warm and honest clasp. But he is too mystified to speak; he calmly waits, expecting an explanation.

'Why don't you speak?' she cries, imploringly. 'Tell me that you do not despise me—that you do not endorse my father's opinion regarding me. He does not trust me—he says that I am not good—that I am wickedly inclined. But tell me that it is not true—tell me that you think him wrong. He does not understand my nature. He cannot read my strangely sensitive disposition, and he judges all my actions wrongly. Ah! God, he has made me suffer! He has made my heart bleed with his reproaches, for he exaggerates my harmless actions into sins. He is harsh, severe, incapable of grasping what is beyond the narrow groove of his experience—and he is my father—alas! he is my father, and . . . .'

'Enough, Miss Forsdyke,' he says, in a strangely agitated voice. 'Do not say another word, I implore you. I comprehend your position thoroughly—every word you say stabs me to the heart. I see now that you are right—it would be impossible to know you well, otherwise

than secretly. Let us bind ourselves together, and swear a friendship on true
platonic lines. Let us be as brother and
sister to one another. Miss Forsdyke, I
thank God that I have been thrown across
your weary path, for I believe that it is
in my power to alleviate your suffering.
Henceforth it shall be my one aim in life
to make you happy—and you must learn
to regard me as a brother, and as a true,
devoted friend.'

He raises her hand to his lips and kisses
it, and with a faint sob she bends her face,
and presses her soft warm lips against his
wrist.

'I will,' she murmurs, 'you shall be
my brother.'

The night-breeze trembles through the
wood, rustling the foliage with a weird
effect. The darkness deepens, wrapping in
obscurity the two sombre figures standing
there together, vowing eternal friendship
to one another; whilst far above them,
through a faint opening in the trees, can be
seen a star faintly twinkling in the purple
sky.

Where are now thy fixed resolves,

Frank Grandby? Where is now thy strength of mind? Gone, vanished, as the last gleams of the setting sun before the hurrying night!

CHAPTER XVI.

VAE VICTIS!

SINCE the night on which the great ladies'
battle was fought across the dinner-service
of Banbury's Hotel, Mrs. Renfrew had not
appeared in public, and it was generally understood that she was confined to her room,
consequent on her having caught a severe
cold on the chest on the morning of the
club dance. She had taken an early walk
with Miss Forsdyke on that morning, so the
report went, and her delicate constitution
had succumbed to the dampness of the
morning mist. Whether there was any
truth or not in the report, no one was in a
position to say for certain, for, in consequence
of Mrs. Renfrew's peculiar reserve, no one in
the hotel had the pleasure of her acquaintance, and no one, strange to say, evinced
any strong desire to make the first overtures

towards the establishment of an intimacy
with the suffering lady. In fact, bearing
their loss with the most exemplary placidity, the inmates of the hotel chatted
and laughed and pursued their different
paths of life, as though there were no such
person as Mrs. Renfrew in existence.

But, to one lady in the hotel, Mrs.
Renfrew's sudden disappearance from the
social circle caused much anxiety and discontent—to wit, Mrs. Stockton, the wife of
Colonel Stockton of the Bengal Cavalry.
And it was neither sympathy nor curiosity
which caused this lady such deep reflections
on the subject; it was merely the thought
that she would be unable to retaliate for the
slight which she had received, until Mrs.
Renfrew chose to emerge from her private
sitting-room. This idea was galling in the
extreme to the cavalry colonel's wife, and
every day which passed without the appearance of her opponent increased her revenge-
ful ire.

She sits for hours, brooding over her late
discomfiture, inwardly cursing her folly for
having been so weak as to have allowed
herself to have been worsted in the encoun-

ter. Daily writhing under this self-inflict-
ed task, her temper becomes unbearable,
resulting in Colonel Stockton suddenly
announcing his determination to proceed
straightway to Kashmir on a shooting ex-
pedition.

'You will do nothing of the sort,' she
answers, shortly. 'As long as I choose to
stay in Doonga, you will remain with me.'

'But, my dear Laura,' expostulates the
colonel, 'I have had no sport this year, and
I need not be absent more than a fortnight.
Surely you can spare me for so short a
time.'

'Spare you!' she ejaculates, contemptuously. 'Don't be a greater fool than nature
was pleased to make you, Colonel Stockton.
I would *spare* you, as you choose to call
it, for a twelvemonth with the greatest
pleasure—if I could only trust you. But
I can't—and the sooner you understand
that fact the better. The idea of a man of
your age wishing to leave his wife, and gad
about the country on the loose! It is
positively disgusting!' and she gives vent
to a sniff of righteous indignation.

'But, my dear Laura,' protested the

colonel, warmly, 'I merely wish to give myself a little innocent amusement. Surely you can see no harm in my having a little shooting in Kashmir?'

'Innocent amusement indeed!' she says, sarcastically. 'That is your idea of innocent amusement, is it?—then we differ, for it is not mine. You can't deceive *me*, Colonel Stockton. I have not lived with you all these years without having framed a pretty accurate estimate of your character—and I know that you are not to be trusted out of my sight for *one* moment. If you had any of the instincts of a husband, you would not wish to leave your wife and home on any pretence whatever. To me the idea is perfectly horrible, you old reprobate!'

'Really, Laura, your language . . .'

'Is only suited to the occasion,' she cries, with an angry toss of her head. 'If you knew your duty as a man and a husband, you would not try to desert your wife at such a moment. Considering how grossly I was insulted at the public dinner-table on Tuesday night, I regard your conduct as infamous and inhuman. If you had a particle of love for me, you would not rest

until you had extracted a full and ample
apology from that—that low, disgusting
female.'

'Oh!' the gallant colonel subsides into a
chair with a low groan.

'That's right!' she cries, with sarcastic
indignation. 'Insult your wife before her
very face! Show her that you are quite
indifferent to her wrongs! Never mind *my*
feelings—I am only a poor helpless woman,
unable to retaliate!'

The colonel covers his face in his hands,
and groans again. The pathetic picture of
his wife's helplessness fails to touch his
hardened heart!

'Why don't you rouse yourself, and show
yourself a man for *once*?' she cries, in tones
of withering contempt. 'Have you *no*
sense of pride in your composition? Can
you sit still and hear your wife—your own
flesh-and-blood, whom you have sworn to
cleave to till separated by death—insulted,
and not offer one word in her defence?
Oh! that I should have lived to see this
day! It would have been better for me,
had I died in early childhood!'

'And for me too,' thinks the colonel,
miserably, expressing his feelings by a

series of low groans. Visions of Kashmir
and peaceful solitudes rise before him in
tantalising contrast to the horror of the
present situation, and he determines not
to yield them up without another struggle.

'But, my dear—my love,' he says, in a
tone of mild expostulation, 'I fancy that
we are wandering from the point. If you
remember, we were discussing my departure
to Kashmir!'

'Understand me once for all, Colonel
Stockton,' she says, leaning towards him,
and shaking her fat finger angrily in his
face. 'You are *not* going to Kashmir alone
—if you want some sport, and are bent on
leaving Doonga, then *1* will accompany
you. I know what you mean to do, you
profligate old villain—you mean to go to
Sarinagar, and *hire a boat!*'

'Hire a boat, my love?' cries the
Colonel, in astonishment. 'What in the
name of wonder should I want a boat for?'

'You can't deceive *me* with your bald
hypocrisy,' she cries, with an angry snort.
'If you think that I don't know why
Sarinagar is so much frequented by the
British officer, you are much mistaken.
Sarinagar has a lake, and on the lake

there are boats to hire, and in those boats the wretches spend the greater portion of their leave.'

'Well, my dear, and if they do—surely it is a most innocent amusement.'

'Fiddle-de-dee! Don't try to get round me,' she cries, contemptuously. 'If you call it an innocent amusement to be rowed about all day by a half-clothed Kashmiri girl....'

'Laura—your language is most outrageous! Do you dare to insinuate that I am capable of such—such horrible—conduct? Have I ever given you cause to suspect me of infidelity?'

'I would sooner not discuss further your reprehensible inclinations,' she answers, sharply. 'I merely repeat my former statement—if you go, I go with you.'

'But, my love—I mean to rough it terribly—to live in a little tent, and cook my own food. I would not think of allowing *you* to undertake such hardships.'

'You are very solicitous for my welfare, I have no doubt!' she says, with a sarcastic snort. 'But you will allow me to be the best judge of my own affairs. Where you go, I, as your wife, mean to follow. If you persist in going to Kashmir, however disagreeable it may be to me to have to yield up all the necessary comforts of life, still I shall do it—I shall accompany you. You will have to find room for *me* in your *little* tent, and you will have to cook *my* dinner in addition to your own—and my appetite is very good. No one shall say that *I* am wanting in my duties as wife, however shamefully I may be neglected. So kindly decide at once, Colonel Stockton, so that I can make all the necessary arrangements. Do you intend to go to Kashmir, or do you not?'

She sits before him grim and terrible. The unfortunate husband springs from his chair with a loud curse.

'No,' he says, ' on such horrible terms, I *won't* go—and—and—may you be damned!' with which delicate little reference to her future state, he leaves the room, slamming the door behind him.

Mrs. Stockton rises with a look of grim satisfaction on her heavy features, feeling that she has scored another victory over her husband, who probably under the instigation of her *bête-noir*, Major Lamb, has of late shown himself inclined to be refractory.

She was one of those unfortunately disposed women, who regard the whole of mankind as their natural enemy—who see in every harmless look and gesture a studied insult, and her pride and dogged perseverance caused and enabled her to follow up all fancied slights with a relentless fury. Her disposition was so thoroughly disagreeable, that her one pleasure in life seemed to be to quarrel with her neighbours. Her capacity for direct aggression was unequalled, and her ability to raise a dispute on every conceivable subject and occasion, to draw the enemy into battle, to force its weak point, to rout and cover it with confusion could only have been acquired by a life-long study. In fact, she was a woman dangerous to the peace and harmony of all communities—a woman devoid of woman's instincts, and capable of conceiving a most insensate hatred against every human creature—a woman to whom the words *love* and *charity* had no significance whatever.

But the one idea predominating in Mrs. Stockton's mind at this moment was the insult which she had received at Mrs. Renfrew's hands, and which she had been unable to wipe out, in consequence of the latter lady's sudden illness. She does not take into consideration that her own behaviour on that occasion might have been more refined and elegant. She totally ignores this little point; in fact, her mind would have been incapable of seeing her conduct in its true light, even had some confiding friend had the temerity to attempt to explain it to her. She only remembers that Mrs. Renfrew, by an exasperating display of calmness, had made her the laughing-stock of the dinner-table; and the thought rankles in her mind like a gangrened sore.

She has no faith at all in the genuineness of Mrs. Renfrew's reported illness; she has brooded over the subject so long that she has thoroughly convinced herself that it is merely a ruse on that lady's part, adopted with the purpose of avoiding contact with her; and she becomes so imbued with this idea that she determines not to rest until she has openly exposed this base imposture of the enemy. Accordingly she sits down and pens a little note to Mrs. Renfrew, couched in terms of the tenderest sympathy, begging to be allowed to pay her a short visit of condolence.

'I trust that you will not take offence at my offer of assistance,' she writes, bending over her desk, with a venomous contraction of the lips. 'It seems so sad to think of you lying there in your room, alone, away from all your friends.'

This she places in an envelope, and gives to a servant, with injunctions to take it to Mrs. Renfrew's room, and to await an answer.

In less than a quarter-of-an-hour the servant returns, bearing a little note, which she eagerly seizes and opens.

'DEAR MRS. STOCKTON,

'My aunt desires me to thank you for your very kind inquiries. She regrets that she is not well enough to take advantage of your kind offer to come and see her.

'Yours sincerely,
'DIANA FORSDYKE.'

That is all! Nothing could be curter and more to the point! No elaboration of words could have conveyed more exactly the meaning intended than these few lines penned by the hand of the fair Diana.

Her offer of sympathy has been rejected! The undercurrent of hypocrisy has been detected beneath her honied phrases, and she has received a rebuff—a stinging enjoinment, glistening with the varnish of social courtesy, to mind her own business!

She crushes the letter in her hand, her face convulsed with impotent anger.

'Tell me,' she cries, in fluent Hindi, 'did you see the lady?'

'Yes, memsahib,' answers the trembling servant. 'There were two memsahibs in the room.'

'And you gave them my letter?'

'I gave the note to the old memsahib. She was lying on a long chair.'

'Yes, you wretch,' she cries, impatiently, 'and what happened?'

'The memsahib opened the *chitti*, read it, and threw it in the fire-place.'

'Well?'

'She laughed, and spoke to the miss-sahib, who sat down and wrote that *chitti*.'

'Tell me the truth, you lying pig! Did the memsahib laugh?'

'Protector of the poor!' says the man, joining the palms of his hands before him in supplication. 'Allah is good! This is the truth! The two memsahibs laughed loudly, and when I went out they laughed again.'

'You may go!'

They had laughed at her! Not only had they seen through her covert scheme, but they had mocked her behind her back, and had gloated over her discomfiture!

This thought rouses all the latent madness in this strange woman's nature. Purple with rage at the consciousness of her defeat, she rises from her seat and stalks about the room. What can she do? How can she retaliate? How can she avenge the insult which she has received?

The clock on the mantelpiece chimes the half-past three, and, still under the influence of her ungovernable temper, she is pacing the room and acting like a madwoman. In her distorted vision the rebuff which she has received becomes magnified into an insult of the gravest order, and, carried away by her anger, she determines to wipe it out at once.

In another moment she is standing outside the door, with her hands resting irresolutely on the handle, looking down the corridor in the direction of Mrs. Renfrew's rooms. She has no fixed purpose in her mind; blinded with impotent rage, she is hardly conscious of her action. Then she leaves the doorway and walks quickly down the passage. She is determined to discover for herself whether Mrs. Renfrew's illness is reality or sham, and, if it proves to be the latter, she is resolved to force an entry and meet her face to face.

Arriving opposite Mrs. Renfrew's door, she pauses a moment to calm the violent beatings of her heart. All is still—the corridor is deserted and no sound of life proceeds from within the room. In the hopes of gaining a view of the interior of the room, she cautiously bends down and applies her eye to the keyhole, but she is disappointed, for the key is in the lock on the other side, and with a look of baffled rage she removes her eye.

Suddenly a faint murmuring of voices strikes upon her ear, and immediately she is all attention. She bends down again and leans her weight against the door, with her ear applied to the key-hole, straining all her powers to catch the purport of the conversation

At first she can distinguish nothing—

only a confused buzz of voices, which appears to proceed from the inner room, which has no outlet on the corridor. Then a word or two strikes upon her ear distinctly, and she redoubles her attention. From the tones of the voices, it seems as though the two ladies were engaged in some slight altercation. She recognises Mrs. Renfrew's plaintive strain, raised apparently in injured complaint, and then follows a soft murmur from Miss Forsdyke, of which the listening woman is unable to detect a single syllable.

Presently Mrs. Renfrew's piping treble travels across the room.

'I am not dissatisfied with you at all, Diana,' it says. 'Of course it is only right that you should take daily exercise, and get some fresh air. I merely wished to impress on you not to stay out too long. A wretched invalid like myself finds the time drag very heavily, if left alone for long.'

And then Miss Forsdyke's voice rises full and clear.

'Ah! dear aunt, I cannot bear to think that you imagine that I could neglect you

for one moment. I owe so much to you
that I should be a wicked girl indeed if I
did not love you dearly. I shall not be
out long. My head is aching from being
confined so long indoors, and I feel inclined for brisk exercise. But I shall certainly be back by six.'

'You are certainly right in saying that
you owe me much,' says Mrs. Renfrew.
'Though your father did not specialise; he
wrote me such a statement of your general
character that I am sure most women
would have thought twice before taking
charge of you.'

'But, aunt, it is not true,' says Miss
Forsdyke, in a pleading tone.

'That I cannot say,' answers Mrs. Renfrew, sharply. 'Your father is a very
religious man, I know—he always was,
even when a child, inclined to Methodism
—and I hardly imagine him capable of
fabricating base aspersions against his only
child. If he does do so, religion must have
sent him mad. However, as a Christian
woman, I am not biassed in the least—I
judge you as I find you, not by hearsay.
Up till now you have been all that is
amiable and good.'

'And I will continue so, my dearest aunt.'

The eager listener at the door exerts every nerve in her body to hear every word of the foregoing conversation. With her hands resting on her knees, she presses her ear tightly against the key-hole, and so violent is the strain resulting from this inclined position, that her face assumes an apoplectic hue. Suddenly the door opens from within, and Mrs. Stockton, completely losing her balance, falls headlong into the room, to the profound amazement of Miss Forsdyke, who has been on the point of going out.

She starts back with a little cry of fright. The violence of the fall has deprived the unfortunate woman of her wind, and she lies on the floor spluttering and snorting, apparently on the verge of apoplexy, and presenting such an extraordinary figure that Miss Forsdyke does not know whether to shriek for help or laugh aloud.

She is recalled to her senses by the aggrieved voice of Mrs. Renfrew coming from the inner room.

'It is really too bad of you,' cry the petulant tones. 'What have you been doing now? You have given my poor nerves such a shock that I shan't forget it for a week.'

But Miss Forsdyke feels unable to move or speak. She stands gazing down at the unwieldy form, gasping spasmodically for breath, in a kind of tranced bewilderment.

'Will you answer me, Diana?' comes Mrs. Renfrew's voice, raised now in high irritation. 'What have you done? Have you broken anything? What is that puffing noise? Is the house on fire, or what? What an aggravating girl you are!'

Still no answer. Mrs. Stockton's sudden and ungraceful entry has so completely paralysed her every movement that, to save her life, she feels she could not say a word.

'Oh! my nerves—my poor nerves!' pipes Mrs. Renfrew, from within; 'what has happened to the girl? Has she been and killed herself, or why does she not answer? Oh! dear me, I am frightened to death! What a noise she is making— it is simply awful! I must go and see! Oh, my nerves, my nerves, I am all of a tremble!'

Miss Forsdyke hears her aunt rise from

her couch and cross the inner room, and then the door of communication opens, and Mrs. Renfrew appears, shaking like an aspen leaf in every limb.

' Diana, where are you ?—Goodness gracious, what is the matter ? What is that upon the floor ?'

Pale with fright, she advances quickly across the room, and bends down over the prostrate figure.

' Mrs. Stockton !' she exclaims, in tones of the deepest amazement ; 'what is she doing here ? Is she ill ? Diana, what does this mean ?'

She looks sharply across at her niece, with a sniff of angry suspicion.

'It was a most extraordinary thing, aunt,' cries Diana, flushed and excited. ' I went to the door and opened it, and immediately Mrs. Stockton fell headlong into the room.'

' *Most* extraordinary, as you say!' answers Mrs. Renfrew, with delicate sarcasm. ' You opened the door, and Mrs. Stockton fell headlong into the room ! What a very strange proceeding on her part, to be sure ! Is the lady hurt ?'

She asks the question in the calmest of

tones, as though she were making some
casual inquiry of polite indifference. It is
wonderful to note how suddenly Mrs. Renfrew's nerves have disappeared under the
excitement of the moment!

'I really cannot say, aunt,' returns
Diana, kneeling down beside the wretched
woman; 'I think that she has merely lost
her breath.'

She bends over Mrs. Stockton and politely asks her whether she be hurt or not.
The latter, puffing and blowing like a
grampus of unusually strong power of lung,
shoots at her a glance of hate, and tries to
speak.

'I—will—pay—you—out—for this,' she
pants, holding both her sides, as though
the effort of speaking were very painful.
'I won't—forget it,—you—mark—my—
words!'

Miss Forsdyke rises flushed and grave.

'There is noting serious the matter with
her, aunt,' she says, quietly; 'she has only
lost her breath for a moment or so.'

'Poor, dear, suffering creature! How
very sad, indeed!' remarks Mrs. Renfrew,
with a fine affectation of sympathy. 'Really, Diana, she requires assistance—she

must not be left in this condition! Send
the *bearer* at once with my compliments to
the manager of the hotel, and request him
to step up here immediately.'

Miss Forsdyke steps out on to the balcony, and gives the message to the native,
who disappears at once to do her bidding.

The manner in which Mrs. Renfrew has
risen to the situation is really admirable.
For a lady who has suffered all her life
from a weakness of the nervous system,
the perfect calmness with which she issues
her orders, and surveys the miserable
woman at her feet, is literally amazing.
She stands in the middle of the room with
nose slightly tilted into the air, and lips
firmly closed, patiently awaiting the advent
of the manager.

Miss Forsdyke is not so calm. There is
a slight flush upon her delicate cheek, and
a trace of excitement in her glance. She
is thinking of the words of menace which
have just fallen from Mrs. Stockton's lips,
and she is vainly trying to account for the
tone of bitter hatred which characterised
the speech.

Mrs. Stockton is still lying full-length
upon the floor, giving no signs of ever

getting up again.   To a lady of her abnormally obese proportions, such a shock as she has received is not by any means a trifle.

The noise of voices is heard approaching from the end of the corridor, and in another moment the manager is bowing himself politely into the room.   On seeing Mrs. Stockton stretched upon the ground, he starts back with an exclamation of dismay; but, before he can speak, Mrs. Renfrew advances towards him, and shows herself mistress of the situation.

'Mr. Banbury,' she says, in a calmly polite tone, 'I regret to say that this unfortunate lady has been guilty of the most dishonourable and unladylike proceeding of eavesdropping at my keyhole.   Unaware of her proximity, my niece suddenly opened the door, and the lady fell forward heavily to the ground.   She is not hurt, I believe—she has merely lost her breath. I must request you, Mr. Banbury, in your capacity of manager of this hotel, to remove the lady immediately from my private apartment.   I must also warn you that, should such an annoyance as this be repeated, I shall feel compelled to leave your hotel.'

She gives him a stately inclination of the head, and walks to her bed-room, closing the door behind her; whilst Miss Forsdyke, repressing an inclination to laugh hysterically at the grotesque absurdity of the whole affair, leaves the room, and hurries off in the direction of the wood, to keep her second appointment with Frank Grandby.

For some moments the manager stands doubtfully viewing the panting lady on the floor. It strikes him forcibly that it will be a matter of no small difficulty to bodily remove a lady of such a magnificent presence as Mrs. Stockton from one room to another. But he does not pause for long—his time is far too precious to allow him to waste it over such an irregular, unbusiness-like proceeding. He hastily collects four or five servants together, and acting under his directions, in spite of her desperate struggles, they manage to lift her from the floor and place her on a sofa. The manager then leads the way, and the natives propel the heavily-weighted piece of furniture down the corridor in the direction of her room.

Slowly moves the funeral-like *cortège !*

Alas ! how are the mighty fallen !

CHAPTER XVII.

UNDER THE TRYSTING-OAK.

THE wise and provident hand of Nature has so ruled it that all excessive strains on the human mind are followed by contrary reactions, which gradually restore the equilibrium of the senses; after a period of intense excitement comes a soothing calm; after protracted grief, a resuscitation of placidity; after killing joy, a state of mild tranquillity—otherwise the human brain would break and die. And this reaction settles heavily on the excited mind of Grandby on awakening on the morning after his meeting with Miss Forsdyke.

Desirous as he is of becoming Miss Forsdyke's intimate friend, he cannot repress his vexation at finding himself placed in so embarrassing a position. His clear sense of honour revolting at the idea of a

secret intimacy, it seems to him, by having
consented to the scheme, that he has been
guilty of a display of weakness degrading
to his manhood.   It is impossible for him
to conceal from himself the fact that this
projected friendship with Miss Forsdyke
bears a terribly close resemblance to a low
intrigue.

To a young man of his high morality
this idea naturally causes much annoyance,
and gives much play for earnest thought.
The venture on which he finds himself
embarked is dead against his inclinations,
and he reproaches himself strongly for not
having remained firm in his resolve.   He
should have manfully resisted all tears
and protestations, and should have refused
point-blank to have had any share in the
illicit scheme.   He should have nerved his
heart to sacrifice all personal desire in the
cause of duty.

This is what he *should* have done!   In
these early hours of the day, with the
brain thoroughly refreshed by a long
night's rest, he sees this plainly.   But
then he did not do it!   Under the excitement of the moment, his firm resolves
had melted like the Himalayan snows in

June before the sun. And therefore he
feels that it is of no avail for him to waste
his time in vain regrets—the die is cast,
and by his hand, and he must now abide
by the result. For he never hesitates one
instant in his intention to fulfil the promise which he has so weakly given.
Though conscious that probably he would
never have consented to the scheme had
not he been labouring under the influence
of an intense excitement, his sense of
honour recoils before the thought of breaking his promised word. He has solemnly
affirmed his intention of becoming her true
and faithful friend on the lines dictated
by herself, and he resolutely determines
to carry out his promise to the letter.

Before separating from Miss Forsdyke
on the evening previously, they had arranged to meet on the morrow at the same time
in the same place, so at a quarter before
the hour of four on this Saturday afternoon Frank Grandby emerges from the
grounds of the hotel and again takes the
road towards the wood. A look of anxiety
overcasts his features as he walks along,
for he finds it impossible to dissipate the
sense of guilt which weighs upon his mind.

But, in spite of this, he is conscious of experiencing deep down in his heart a sense of soft contentment at the prospect of finding himself once again in the society of Miss Forsdyke. That his interest in her personality is slowly and surely on the increase he is only too well aware, for she never leaves his thoughts—from morning till night he finds himself, half-unconsciously, dwelling on the details of her *petite* form and strange sombre existence; and he views his conduct in this particular with a feeling of semi-wonderment, for such a proceeding on his part is quite foreign to his usual line of conduct.

Four years before, a great blow had fallen on his life. His only sister, whom he had worshipped with a passionate devotion, had died in India, where she had proceeded on her marriage. At the early age of eighteen she had married a man who had been in no way worthy to possess her. He was a handsome, idle, worthless young fellow, as unstable as water, and possessing more money than common-sense, and, from the first moment that she set her eyes upon his god-like face, she loved him with a love which became the passion of her life. And he, too, for his part became deeply enamoured of the pure young girl, and day after day would ride over from the barracks, where he was quartered, to look upon her winsome face. In her sweet presence the knowledge of his own self-degradation would strike him to the heart, and, on the day when they interchanged their vows of love, he solemnly swore to her to purge himself of all vice and wickedness, and to reform.

There was much opposition to their union. At first Mrs. Grandby would not hear of it being mentioned; the life of profligacy which he had led was known to all the world, and she—good, loving mother—shrank from the idea of her daughter mating with a reprobate. But he seemed so thoroughly in earnest in his intention to reform, and he pleaded so strongly for her consent, with the tears glistening in those deep-blue eyes of his, which were found so strangely hard to resist by all, that finally she yielded, and agreed to accept him as a son-in-law, on the understanding that the marriage should not take place at least for another year, during which he was to prove to her and the

U

world at large that he was worthy to possess her daughter.

Frank Grandby at this time was in his seventeenth year, and he became a firm champion of his sister's cause, for it was impossible not to like the man she loved. He was not bad—he was merely weak, and Frank boy-like viewed all his faults with a lenient eye, feeling assured in his heart that he was genuine in his resolve to lead a better life. And so two months went by, and, under the influence of his love, young Talbot became another man.

At the end of that period, his regiment received sudden orders to depart for India, and Mrs. Grandby's tender heart could not resist the earnest supplications of the young couple. She gave her consent to an immediate marriage, and, a week before the regiment sailed, they were bound together in holy matrimony in the little parish church. A year passed, and then came the painful news of the young wife's sudden death—she had died of enteric fever contracted in one of the hill-stations of the Himalayas.

Frank Grandby's grief was terrible. He had loved his sister more than any other human soul on earth, and the news of her death was a shock from which he never totally recovered. From that moment something was wanting in his life; there was a void in his heart which he felt could never be refilled.

The knowledge that his sister's married life had been one short dream of happiness, somewhat lessened the poignancy of his sorrow; for Charlie Talbot had been true to his promise, and had never given her cause for a moment's pain. The last letter which she had written to him had been full of touching allusions to the great tenderness of her husband's love.

Charlie Talbot had written, announcing the death of his wife. It was as pathetic and heart-breaking an epistle as perhaps has ever been penned by human hand. It was evident that he was completely crushed by the magnitude of his sorrow. Frank wrote to him in reply a letter full of tender sympathy. 'Within a year's time,' he wrote, ' I hope I shall clasp your hand in mine.' But it was fated that they should never meet again. Before Grandby started for India, the news arrived of Talbot's sudden death. Travelling in the wilds of

Kashmir, he had met with an awful death : he had fallen over a precipice and had been smashed upon the rocks beneath.

Grandby allowed many a sigh to escape him, thinking over the death of his handsome brother-in-law. He never could forget the fact that it was owing to Charlie Talbot that the last year of his sister's life had been crowned with such perfect happiness ; and it had made no difference in his regard for him, when vague rumours came across the seas that he had again returned to his old life of profligate folly. With the death of his good spirit, it was said that Talbot had again succumbed to that fatal weakness of mind which had been his curse through life. Mention of his name was made in scandalous connection with more than one woman, and it was even whispered that there was a lady in some way or other mysteriously interwoven with the cause of his fearful death. But Grandby never took the trouble to inquire into the truth of these reports. Loyal to the memory of his friend, he only thought of him in his character of a devoted husband to his dead, beloved sister.

Four years had elapsed since that sad

morning when the mail brought the news of his sister's death, and still Grandby had not recovered from the wound it caused him. No woman had ever arisen to fill up that dreary gap in his affections caused by her sudden loss. And now, as he walks along on this autumn afternoon to keep his assignation, the thought strikes him that possibly, by a gracious act of Providence, Miss Forsdyke has been thrown across his path with this set purpose.

He ponders over this idea, and it does not strike him as impossible. The strangeness of his sudden interest in the girl only tends to verify the notion. It seems to him that that subtle bond of sympathy which exists between them is a proof that it was ordained that they should meet and be more to one another than casual acquaintances. And, by some irresistible unknown influence, such in fact had been effected. They have met, and, acting under the directions of the same unknown power, they have sworn to one another a vow of friendship; they have entered on a contract of platonic love and fraternal confidence; they have arranged to stand to one another in the relationship of brother to sister.

The strange idea gains ground on his heated imagination; the more he ponders, the more he becomes convinced that he is right in his belief that it is ordained that Miss Forsdyke should take that place in his affections formerly occupied by his sister. And in accepting this belief, he experiences no pain at the thought of another occupying the shadowed void; it does not strike him that such a contingency would be a sacrilege to the sacred memory of his buried love: it merely fills him with a sensation of ineffable joy and surpassing contentment. For in Miss Forsdyke he sees not a totally distinct individuality, but the living spirit of his sister embodied in a different form, and through this new embodiment can be gained access to that gentle spirit which he formerly knew and loved so well.

Musing thoughtfully over this idea, he reaches the spot of assignation. Miss Forsdyke has not yet arrived. Only the huge oak, with its heavy outstretched bough, against which they had leaned the day before, confronts him, and he walks towards it, and prepares to wait patiently for her arrival by taking out a cigarette and lighting it.

The same hushed calm pervades the wood; the trees, as yet untinged with autumnal yellow, raise their rich foliage in silence to the sky. The trysting-oak, near which he is standing, rises from a knoll of soft, green turf, with masses of maiden-hair fern clustering about its roots. It is a tree of colossal size, plainly showing by its hollow trunk the ravages of time, and presenting a striking contrast, in its rugged gnarled appearance, to those in its immediate vicinity. Round its trunk, with a gradual inclination downwards, the green turf stretches until it reaches on every side a thick growth of fern, with violet, white, and yellow balsam intermixed, extending in all directions as far as the eye can reach. It is a pretty little fairy spot, rising like an island out of the surrounding sea of undergrowth—a veritable inspiration on the part of Dame Nature—and Grandby, lazily puffing the thin white coils of smoke and watching them gradually disperse in the balmy air, experiences a sense of calm enjoyment from the beauty of his surroundings.

The moments pass, and still no Miss Forsdyke comes. He moves towards the tree, and leans his arms across the bough, and gazes up in a kind of dreamlike ecstacy at the small patch of blue sky discernible through the trees.

He is aroused from his reverie by the touch of a soft hand upon his arm, and, quickly looking round, he sees Miss Forsdyke standing beside him with a vivid colour on her cheeks.

'I have come so fast,' she says, with a little laugh, shaking him by the hand, ' that I have quite lost my breath. Am I very late? I am afraid that I have kept you waiting very long.'

He eagerly returns the soft pressure of her hand. Her heightened colour enhances the delicate beauty of her face, and he looks into her laughing eyes with a thrill of admiration. All trace of sorrow has disappeared from her charming countenance; as she stands before him, she looks the very picture of light-hearted gaiety.

'We have had such an adventure,' she cries, breathlessly. 'Mrs. Stockton has been lying on our floor, puffing and blowing like an inverted steam-engine. The old wretch must have been listening at our keyhole. I was on the point of starting to come here, and, on opening our sitting-room door, she suddenly fell headlong into the room. You may imagine my consternation at her unexpected and peculiar entry! It was really no joke at first, I can tell you, for she lay on the floor panting and wheezing to such an extent that I really believed her to be on the point of death.'

'What an extraordinary occurrence! What on earth did you do?' he asks, smiling at her childlike excitement.

'Oh! it was really most laughable—for she was not hurt a bit, you know. The force of the fall had taken away her breath, and the poor old thing could not articulate. one word. My aunt, who is, as you know, confined to her room with *nerves*,' she continues, with a comical expression on her face, 'came limping in, with her cap all awry, and pale with fright, and soon settled the business. She rang for the manager, and told him to remove the woman at once. How he managed to do it I can't conceive, for I immediately seized on the chance of escape and hurried off—but she is no mean weight, is she?'

A clear, merry laugh rings through the stillness of the wood.

'You can have no idea,' she cries, 'what an absurd spectacle she presented, lying huddled on the floor. I feel that I could laugh at the recollection till I cried. What I should have done had my aunt not been present, goodness only knows! Probably I should have fallen down beside her in a similar state of helplessness. But isn't it awful to think of her being guilty of such a low trick?' she adds, her voice assuming a tone of gravity. 'Fancy a woman in her position demeaning herself to such an extent as to eavesdrop at our door.'

'I can hardly conceive it possible,' answers Grandby, in a tone of blank amazement. 'What *could* have been her motive.'

'I really cannot say,' she answers, thoughtfully, 'unless it be that she bears a grudge against my aunt for having made those unfortunate remarks at dinner last Tuesday. But that is hardly probable, is it?'

'Do you know Mrs. Lamb—that faded yellow woman?' he asks. 'Well, she warned me very strongly not to offend Mrs. Stockton. She told me that she was

vindictive almost to madness, and would
never forgive a slight, however small. So
perhaps your suggestion may be right.'

'My aunt is a perfect judge of character,
and she seems to have been of the same
opinion. Before this mishap occurred,
Mrs. Stockton wrote a little note of condolence to my aunt, asking to be allowed to
come and see her, and, without a moment's
consideration, Mrs. Renfrew dictated to me
a curt refusal, saying, as she did so, that
she was not quite such a fool as Mrs. Stockton presumably supposed her to be. So
it seems as if she distrusted her, doesn't
it?'

'Yes, certainly,' he replies. 'It is unfortunate, that we should have both incurred
this aggressive old woman's spite. After
I refused to dance with her, she cast on
me such a glance of hate that I half suspected the venom of her character.'

'But, Mr. Grandby,' she cries, with a
ringing laugh, 'you do not really mean
to tell me that she actually asked you to
dance?'

'I assure you that she did,' he laughs, in
reply.

'And you were so ungallant as to refuse!

Oh—fie—Mr. Grandby! I really thought better of you than that.'

'But surely you will admit, that there was some excuse for my behaviour? Imagine me walking disconsolately about that ball-room, vainly attempting to fathom the mystery of a certain little scented *billet-doux*, which . . . . . .'

'Yes, you may well pause!' she answers, blushing modestly; 'I presume your conscience is pricking you for alluding to such a disgraceful episode.'

'It wasn't disgraceful at all!' he retorts, stoutly. 'You acted under the impulse of the moment, and—and I am devoutly thankful to think you did. Do you know, Miss Forsdyke, that to-day I have been struck with a very strange idea?'

'No—have you?' she says, opening her eyes in innocent wonderment. 'Do—please —confide it to me. But supposing we sit down. There is no reason why we should stand here like talking dummies. This grassy slope seems made for weary limbs.'

He readily agrees, and they both sink down on to the soft green turf, side by side. He is charmed with the open, sisterly manner in which she has treated him to-day.

Under its influence, all sense of embarrassment has flown, and he feels as much at
his ease with her as if he had known her
all her life.

'And now tell me your idea,' she says,
sitting up, with her hands folded prettily
on her lap, and with an air of expectant interest on her sunny little countenance.

'Well, first you must promise not to
laugh at me,' he says, with some hesitation,
looking her shyly in the face.

'Laugh at you!' she says, in astonishment. 'Of course I shall not laugh at you.
You ought to know me better than even
to think of such a thing.'

'I only thought that the idea which
seems so possible to me might strike you
as ridiculous,' he says, in half-apologetic
tones. 'And it involves such a very serious
question that I could not bear you laughing at it.'

'Of course, I will not laugh,' she answers,
softly. 'Tell me, what is it?'

'Well, you must know,' he answers, in a
low voice, 'that four years ago I suffered
a terrible loss. My darling sister, whom I
had loved with a passionate devotion, died.
She was the only creature, save my mother,

whom I had ever had to love—and consequently my love for her was all the
stronger.   And, when she died, I thought
that happiness had gone out of my life for
ever.   But I was young then, and did not
understand that time can partially heal
every wound.   You follow me?'

With a grave inclination of the head,
she silently assents. 'And time in my
case has done wonders,' he continues, ' but
it has never wholly healed the wound, and
I am certain that it never will.   There is
something wanting in my life of which I
am ever conscious—a dreary sense of in-
completeness which I can never dissipate.
I know that my life has been embittered
by her sudden death, and I know that it is
the memory of my loss which makes my
disposition so painfully reserved.'

'Yes,' she murmurs, sympathically,
' you interest me deeply.'

' Do I ?' he asks, with a sudden animation. ' It makes me very happy to think so,
for it partially confirms the strange idea,
with which I was seized this afternoon.   It
is so seemingly impossible, so—so—un-
realizable, that I hardly know how I can

put it into words, so as to make it clear to you.'

'Ah—try!' she murmurs. 'Only try!—I feel intuitively that I shall understand your meaning.'

'Well, it is this,' he says, lowering his voice almost to a whisper. 'I have been seized with the idea that possibly—possibly, my sister's spirit has—has returned to this world, to live with me again in personal communion.'

'What!' she cries, unable to repress her intense astonishment, 'what *do* you—Ah, Mr. Grandby, explain to me your meaning clearly—as yet I do not understand.'

Her voice again assumes a tone of tender sympathy, and she bends forward with a gesture amounting almost to a caress, a look of eager inquiry in her face. He notes the sudden ring of astonishment in her voice, and continues in a more excited tone.

'Do you not understand me?' he cries. 'Something within me tells me that my sister's spirit has returned again, embodied in a different form. I cannot shake off the strange idea, and every moment

which passes makes me more and more
convinced that I am right.   As I sit here
and look at you, and talk to you, and hear
you talk to me, it seems to me impossible
that it can be otherwise than that.'

She looks up suddenly, with a flush of
warm colour sweeping across her skin.
The air of puzzled bewilderment which she
has worn for the last few minutes disappears, giving place to an expression of
joyous triumph which she is unable wholly
to repress.   Her emotion is so great that
for a moment she finds herself incapable
of speaking.   Then, with an effort, she con-
trols herself, and speaks in trembling tones.

' Do I understand you right ?' she says,
her voice sinking to a whisper, ' do you
refer to me when you speak of your sister's
spirit ?'

'Yes,' he answers, in an agitated voice,
' I refer to you.   Does the notion strike
you as absurd ?   Do you fully comprehend
my meaning ?'

' Do I resemble her in any way ?' she
asks, in the same hushed tone.

'Not in looks—nor in manners,' he answers, quickly.   ' It is not that I mean.
It is the fact of my having conceived for

you such a wondrous sympathy, that has given me the idea. From the very first moment that I set eyes upon you, I became conscious of feeling a deep interest in your person, and from that moment till now that interest has been growing hour by hour, stronger and stronger, until it has reached that point which compels me to regard you as a sister. To-day I recognised that the feeling which you have inspired in me is closely akin to the love I bore my sister—never before have I been conscious of anything resembling it. Ah, Diana—Miss Forsdyke, do you think that there can possibly be any truth in this strange idea, or do you think that weakness of body has made me fanciful?'

In his excitement he leans forward and takes her by the hand. Again, unperceived by him, the same expression of triumphant joy sweeps across her downcast face. With a gentle pressure of the hand, she turns her eyes towards his anxiously expectant face.

'Frank,' she murmurs, softly,—'for, feeling as we do towards one another, why should we adopt a formal method of address,—the idea which you have propounded to me is too abstruse for my poor feeble intellect to follow or to discuss. I have no power to tell you whether you be right or wrong—I only know that I feel towards you the same feeling of fraternal regard as you admit you feel for me. Why I do so I cannot tell—I do not understand the matter. There seems to be some mysterious influence drawing me towards you —an influence so strong that it is impossible for my weak mind to stand against it. If what you suggest could really be, then it would readily account for my great regard for you. Whether it could be or not, I cannot venture to say—I have never thought upon such subjects. But I do not see why it should *not* be true. Ah! if I could only believe in it—then everything which is now so mysterious would be plain to me.'

'Then believe, Diana!' he cries, still retaining her hand within his grasp, 'trust to my intuition, and believe! It is true —I know it is—every pulse-beat in my body tells me so. Ah! Diana—Diana!' he says, drawing closer towards her, 'henceforth we must be all in all to one another, for you are my sister, and I am your brother. We must have no secrets from

one another, no joys nor sorrows, which
we must not share together. Diana!
speak to me, and tell me that all I say
strikes a sympathetic chord within your
heart.'

A wave of agitation sweeps across her
face, and her head sinks gently down upon
his shoulder.

' All in all to one another !' she faintly
whispers, ' yes, Frank, we must henceforth
be all in all—from this day a new life
begins—for both of us.'

There is a silence for several minutes
throughout the darkening wood. Both he
and she are conscious of the beatings of
the other's heart, but neither speaks a
word. Then suddenly he bends his head,
and gently touches her forehead with his
lips.

She rises with a hurried start, and
through the deepening twilight he can
discern the rich flush of colour which over-
spreads her face.

' How late it is !' she says, with a fever-
ish excitement. ' I must be going—to-
morrow again at four ?'

' Yes, at four !'

' Good-night, Frank.'

' Good-night, Diana.'

She stands for a moment holding him by the hand, gazing wistfully up into his face, and then she turns away and leaves him alone under the giant oak, already wrapped in the shades of night.

CHAPTER XVIII.

BESIDE HIS SISTER'S GRAVE.

THE next day is Sunday, and, as is the custom with indifferent Christians in these days, Grandby determines to go to church, more from force of habit than from inclination.

So accordingly, having partaken of a late breakfast, he saunters leisurely down the hill towards the little gothic church standing on the Mall. The sacred edifice is crammed to overflowing, but he manages to find a vacant seat. Mrs. Lamb is presiding at the harmonium, and, as he looks towards her, a glance of recognition lightens up her faded face. All Doonga have assembled together to say their prayers. The feminine element, however, strongly predominated—as is usually the case with tea-fights, musical soirées, and public worship

—and it was wonderful to note the extraordinary expression of sanctity with which each one took stock of her neighbour's bonnet and general apparel. It is needless to say that the club was not represented; to those wearied spirits, Sunday was indeed a day of rest.

Neither Mrs. Renfrew nor Miss Forsdyke is present amongst the congregation, and Grandby rightly concludes that the former lady's nerves are not in a fit state to allow her to take part in anything so exciting as the morning service of the Church of England. Mrs. Stockton is also absent, and many whispered comments on her nonappearance run throughout the Banbury contingent; for, sad to relate, that lady's unfortunate mishap of the day before has given rise to the circulation of the most grave aspersion on her character. It has, in fact, been said that she was seen on the preceding afternoon being carried to her room in a state of the most hopeless intoxication.

How the report arose no one could explain, but, notwithstanding this doubt as to its origin and authenticity, it was received with a general satisfaction, and Mrs.

Lamb, for one, was thoroughly convinced that it was true. In fact, at breakfast on this Sunday morning, carried away by the excitement of the occasion and taking advantage of the absence of her enemy, she had openly declared that she had long suspected Mrs. Stockton to possess a partiality for strong liquor; which statement on her part, however, it is only fair to say, was received with caution by her audience.

The service drones through its appointed course, and not even the strange vagaries of the harmonium under Mrs. Lamb's unpractised touch can awaken the congregation to anything like enthusiasm. By the time the clergyman mounts the pulpit-steps the look of apathetic weariness depicted on every face has changed into the more comfortable, but less pleasing one of somnolence. Ladies nod and awake with little frightened starts, fair heads droop on to well-shaped shoulders, and Mrs. Andrews opens her mouth to its widest extent and deliberately and composedly snores.

Grandby, for his part, is hardly conscious of his surroundings, so occupied is he with his own private train of thought. Mechanically he rises, kneels, and sits, according to the rubric, displaying a face lost in religious ecstasy. It can safely be asserted that he does not inwardly digest one word of the preacher's impassioned discourse. Here and there a word or sentence strikes upon his inattentive ear. He has a vague notion that he is being threatened with the tortures of an eternal fire unless he speedily repents, but he bears the thought with a philosophical equanimity, having a strong suspicion that he has heard something very similar to this before; which remark, it may be stated, equally applies to the mass of the congregation present, to judge from the listless apathy depicted on their faces.

It is a very terrible thing to have to write, but it is none the less true, that the greater portion of those assembled are thinking more of their approaching lunch than of their chance of eternal condemnation. It is melancholy also to have to record the sudden look of animation which spreads throughout the building when the padrè turns his back and mumbles inarticulately in the direction of the altar. Then what a change comes o'er the spirit of the edifice! What a sudden rising and rustling of silks and satins down the aisle!

What an interchange of little nods and smiles and endless pretty coquetries! What a startling wakening from apathy to life! File out, fair Christians, from the porch! Your weekly spell of martyrdom is over, and your elastic consciences may now remain at rest for seven whole days!

The harmonium bursts into a triumphal march, and the discords rise with such surprising audacity from the blurred, wheezing tones of the ancient instrument that even Grandby, in spite of his preoccupation of mind, cannot fail to notice them. There is a smile of amusement on his face, as he glances in its direction, and he nearly laughs outright at the ludicrous aspect presented by Mrs. Lamb, with her shoulders raised up to her ears, and her body distorted into unexpected angles. He passes out into the bright sunshine, and stands for several moments watching those around him.

Presently a hand is laid upon his arm, and, turning round, he finds himself face to face with Mrs. Lamb. He courteously raises his hat, and shakes her by the hand.

' I wanted to speak to you so much, Mr. Grandby,' she says, with a coquettish wriggle of the neck, ' that I had to leave off

most abruptly in the march from " Athalie "
—a lovely thing, isn't it, so effective on a
wind instrument—for fear of not catching
you.   Where do you hide yourself all day?
I see so little of you that I can hardly
fancy we are staying at the same hotel !'

' You flatter me by confessing to having
remarked my absence,' he says, with a
pleasant smile.   ' I am afraid I am not what
you call a *ladies' man.*   I like the seclusion
of my own room, surrounded by my books.'

' What a very ungallant speech to make!'
she cries, with a sprightly little laugh.
'But you hardly ever even appear at meals
now ?'

'I always appear when I can,' he answers.
' As a rule, I must admit I am either late
or absent.   I take long walks by myself,
and I never notice how the time passes, and
then if I am very late, I take my dinner in
my room.   But I will really promise you
to be more punctual in future.'

' But walking by yourself must be very
dreary sort of work,' she says.   'You should
find some one to accompany you.   I saw
you leaving the hotel grounds yesterday
about four o'clock, and I felt quite sorry for
your being alone.'

'Oh! really, Mrs. Lamb, you must not say such things, or you will make me quite conceited,' he returns, with a merry laugh. 'Had I but known that my movements were being observed by a fair lady from her lattice window, I am afraid that I should not have walked so composedly as I did. I am quite a stranger in Doonga, and I really enjoy a solitary walk. With such enchanting scenery as this around me, I could never feel dull.'

'Ah! I envy you the pleasure,' she says, with a little sigh. 'I wish that I were strong enough to take long walks. But you must really emerge from your hermit's cell, and be a little more sociable. I shall always be glad to offer you a cup of tea any day about five o'clock, if you choose to drop in and see me!'

'You are very kind, Mrs. Lamb. You may be sure that I shall avail myself of your offer!'

'Mind you do!' she says, playfully shaking her finger towards him. 'And, Mr. Grandby,'—dropping her voice to a confidential whisper—'have you heard of this disgraceful report concerning our joint enemy, Mrs. Stockton?'

'No—what report?'

'Why—they say that yesterday she was found in the corridor in a state of inebriation, and that the manager had to lift her on to a sofa, and to cart her bodily to her room. Have you ever heard of anything so disgraceful, and so—so—delightfully exciting? I declare that my blood has been tingling all the morning at the bare thought of such a thing.'

'What a pity that such a romantic rumour is not true!' says Grandby, smiling. 'It seems quite a shame to be compelled to contradict such a very excellent story.'

'But it is true,' she says, confidently. 'I heard it on the very *best* authority.'

'Well—I am quite loth to undeceive you,' he says, still laughing. 'But I can assure you that it is not true. The unfortunate lady fell down and lost her breath, and that was the reason of her undignified conveyance down the corridor.'

'Oh! but it is impossible, Mr. Grandby,' she says, incredulously. 'Who could have told you that?'

'I heard it from the very best of sources,'

he answers, lightly, 'from one, in fact, who witnessed the whole occurrence.'

'And who was that?' she asks, breathlessly.

'I heard it from Miss Forsdyke.'

The next moment, he is conscious of his mistake. A vivid colour illumines his olive skin, accompanied by a look of the deepest embarrassment.

'From Miss Forsdyke?' she says, in a tone of surprise, noting his confusion. 'Why, I never knew that you were acquainted with that young lady. How on earth did you come to know her? She is not on speaking terms with another soul in Banbury's.'

'I made her acquaintance at the dance,' he stammers, feeling the situation extremely awkward. 'And yesterday a—a chance *rencontre* in the hotel gardens brought us together again. And, yes, I can assure you, Mrs. Lamb,' he continues, rapidly, attempting to change the conversation, 'that it is just as I tell you with regard to Mrs. Stockton. She was standing outside Mrs. Renfrew's door, and it was suddenly opened from within, and she fell headlong into the room. I do not pretend to say what she was doing there.'

' You—you don't mean to say—oh! Mr. Grandby, is it possible?' she cries, clasping her hands together rapturously, and quite forgetting in her excitement her momentary suspicion. ' Oh! how delightful! Why—*your* version of the story is a thousand times more exciting than my own! Only fancy —listening at the keyhole! Could anything be more lovely? But *really* I am not a bit surprised—the woman is capable of any crime.'

' Oh! Mrs. Lamb, you must not jump at conclusions in that audacious manner,' he answers, laughingly. ' Perhaps the poor lady was studying the grain of the wood, or the mechanism of the lock—we must give her the benefit of the doubt. And now, I am afraid, I really must be going. I've something particular to do to-day— and, by-the-by, perhaps you could kindly assist me. Could you direct me to the cemetery?'

'The cemetery!' she exclaims with a start back of affected astonishment. ' Is the hermit going to meditate amongst the dead?'

' No,' he answers, his tone changing suddenly to one of gravity. ' My sister was buried here, and I wish to see her grave.'

' I beg your pardon,' she says, in a tone of sympathetic apology, ' I did not know, or I would not have joked on such a subject. Yes, certainly, I can point you out the way. It is not very far—especially to one who is so fond of walking.'

She gives him a few directions as to which roads to take, and then, with a reminder of his promise to come and see her, she shakes him by the hand, and they separate—she taking the road to Banbury's ; he starting off in the opposite direction down the hill.

He is filled with vexation at having so thoughtlessly mentioned Miss Forsdyke's name, for he is conscious that he has not acted rightly towards the girl in doing so. The peculiar relationship which existed between them did not warrant him referring publicly to her person. He knows that, in order to preserve her good name, the utmost secrecy is necessary, and he curses his folly for not having been more careful with his tongue. However, he consoles himself with the thought that apparently Mrs. Lamb suspected nothing ; but, at the same time, he resolutely determines to be more careful for the future. Another slip of the tongue, such as this, might be the means of exposing the whole affair; and such a contingency might possibly involve Miss Forsdyke in social ruin.

He cannot conceal from himself that, in yielding to her wish, he has entered upon a very desperate game. Under her influence, and under the influence also of his own strange ideas concerning his connection with Miss Forsdyke, the prickings of his own conscience have been quelled. He is fully conscious of the nature of his regard for her; he views her with a calm, brotherly affection, and he knows that, through him, no harm can come to her. But, on the other hand, he is fully alive to the dangers which might possibly arise from external sources. He sees plainly that, should their secret meetings be discovered and exposed, it would be a work of the greatest difficulty to allay the tongues of scandal. His knowledge of the world is sufficient to tell him that it would be no easy task to convince the social world that his friendship with Miss Forsdyke was of a purely platonic character. No man or woman would be found to credit such an explanation. Nothing would ever induce them to believe that a young man and woman, both of exceptionally prepossessing exteriors, and totally disconnected with one another, would agree after one week's acquaintanceship to meet secretly in the secluded depths of a deserted wood solely for the purpose of interchanging ideas of fraternal significancy. The notion was too absurd to be entertained for one instant, and he is so fully alive to the fact that he determines for the future always to be on his guard, and never for one moment to forget that he holds the honour and good name of a pure young girl in his keeping.

Thinking on these matters, and following almost mechanically Mrs. Lamb's directions, he arrives at the gate of the cemetery, through which he passes. The next quarter-of-an-hour he spends in searching for his sister's grave.

He finds it at last in a corner of the enclosure under the shadow of a stalwart tree—a plain slab of grey marble, carved with the following inscription :

Sacred to the Memory of
ADELAIDE MARY,
The beloved wife of CHARLES TALBOT,
Lieutenant 8th Dragoon Guards,
Who departed this life at Doonga,
On June 3rd, 1879,
Aged nineteen years and five months.
' *The Lord giveth and the Lord taketh away.*'

A rush of irresistible tenderness overcomes him, and he sinks down upon his knees beside the cold stone, his eyes suffused with tears. The face and form of his beloved sister rise vividly before him. He sees her again as she appeared to him that last time on which he had set eyes upon her. Then she had been young and full of life, with the rich bloom of a new-born happiness resting on her cheeks—then she had been his flesh and blood, his sister, whom he had worshipped second to none on earth.

And now, what is she? Where is now her youth and happiness, that well-known voice, those kindly eyes, those ever-sympathising tones? Where is now that loving face which hung over him, passionately kissing him, when she said her last good-bye? What now remains to him of her who was once all in all to him?

Nothing! nothing! Only the memory of what once had been, and this cruel slab of marble, with its poignant lettering.

A torrent of hot salt tears bursts from his eyes, and he bends down and passionately kisses her beloved name.

'Adelaide, Adelaide, my darling sister!' he cries, 'can you see me kneeling here?

Look down on me, and see me prostrated by your grave. My little sister—my darling little sister—why have you gone from me so soon? Why did you forsake me, and leave me to fight this dreary world alone?'

For some moments his sorrow completely overcomes him, and his tears flow freely, without an attempt on his part to restrain them. Then by degrees the violence of his agitation subsides, and he rises with a sense of great calm stealing upon him.

She has gone—gone from him for ever! No tears, no lamentations can ever bring her back to him. She has left the world, and gone to a happier sphere, where sorrow is unknown.

Why should he weep? Why should he regret her, and pour out his heart in idle tears? Why should he yearn for her return? Is she not far happier as she is than she would have been had she remained on earth?

He raises his face to heaven, and there is a half smile of tenderness on his lips.

'Adelaide,' he whispers, 'look down on me and guide me. Be my guardian angel, and shed thy holy influence on my life!'

The grave is scrupulously clean and

neat, and now, in his calmer state of mind, he notices the fact, and inwardly thanks the authorities for their care. Suddenly he becomes aware of something which has hitherto escaped his notice. It is a wreath of flowers lying on the ground, touching the grave-stone head. He bends over it and closely examines it, and, to his astonishment, discovers that the flowers—*gloire-de-Dijon* roses of a striking beauty—are still unfaded. Filled with wonder, he lays the wreath back upon the stone.

Who could have placed it on his sister's grave? Who could there be in Doonga who loved her well enough still to reverence her memory? Surely, he thinks, it cannot be the custom of the cantonment authorities to place fresh flowers on the graves.

With the purpose of ascertaining this, he turns round and views the adjacent tomb, and he finds a similar wreath of flowers lying at its head; but he hardly notices them, so riveted are his eyes on the inscription of the stone.

'Sacred to the Memory of
CHARLES TALBOT, Lieutenant 8th Dragoon Guards,
Who met his death by an accident
In Kashmir,
July 8th, 1880.   Aged twenty-seven years.'

'Can it be possible?' he murmurs, half aloud. 'How comes it that Charlie was buried here beside his wife?'

This is the first intimation that he has ever received as to his brother-in-law's last resting-place. Charlie Talbot had died in the northern wilds of Kashmir, and Grandby had always imagined that he had been buried there. That he had been brought these many miles into Doonga had never entered into his conception.

'Who could have done it?' he muses. 'Who could have brought his body all that way, and had him buried beside his wife?'

He bends down and examines the wreath of flowers, having first ascertained that these two graves were the only two thus decorated. It is identical with the one on his sister's tomb. Wondering more and more, he reverentially lays it down, and with a last fond look prepares to leave the cemetery.

'Who could have done it?' he murmurs thoughtfully, as he turns homewards; 'and what kind friend can there be in Doonga who tends their graves so lovingly? How can I ascertain? Ah!—a happy thought—perhaps Loftus will be able to give me some information on the subject.'

END OF THE FIRST VOLUME.

LONDON: PRINTED BY DUNCAN MACDONALD, BLENHEIM HOUSE.